Le

MW01380711

A Spicy MM Novella

G. EILSEL

Letters to Satan

Copyright © 2024 G. Eilsel

All rights reserved.

No part of this book may be reproduced in any form or by any electronic or mechanical means, including information storage and retrieval systems, without written permission from the author, except for the use of brief quotations.

ASIN: 9798300080747

This is a work of fiction. Names, characters, businesses, places, events, locales, and incidents are either the products of the author's imagination or used in a fictitious manner. Any resemblance to actual persons, living or dead, or actual events is purely coincidental.

The author acknowledges the trademark status and trademark owners of various brands, products, and/or restaurants referenced in this work of fiction. The publication or use of these trademarks is not authorized, associated with, or sponsored by the trademark owners.

G. Eilsel

*This one is dedicated to those on the Naughty List.
The ones who saw Santa Daddy and said, "Sign me the fuck up."*

If you're following the count, the word "cock" is used 85 times, this time over 160 pages.

You're welcome.

Letters to Satan

G. Eilsel

BEFORE YOU GET STARTED...

You've found your way to my smutty novella series, and I don't know whether to say thank you or apologize in advance. It can get a little weird in here, y'all.

A few things to make note of:

This is an erotic, 18+ novella with minimal plot, ridiculous humor, and a whole lot of smut.

The sex depicted in this novella may not always be realistic, but that's part of the fun. Allow yourself to just be okay with the fact that stamina is high and refractory periods might be non-existent.

The length of these novellas means that there is always some level of insta-lust to insta-love involved, because since the sex is the plot, we're not devoting a lot of time to relationship building.

TLDR: It's nasty up in here. Have fun.

Letters to Satan

G. Eilsel

TRIGGER WARNINGS

The nature of this novella as a smutty read means there are few triggers that don't have something to with sex. I've included a Shopping List on the next page that breaks down the majority of the kinks and acts included. Despite my best efforts, it's possible I missed something.

Other possible triggering matter that heeds mentioning, even if it's duplicated on the next page:

Death of a parent (in the past, discussed on page)

Letters to Satan

G. Eilsel

SHOPPING LIST

- ❏ Oral sex
- ❏ Cum play
- ❏ Daddy kink (no LB/Age play)
- ❏ Domination
- ❏ Submission
- ❏ Degradation
- ❏ Begging
- ❏ Praise
- ❏ Impact play
- ❏ Minor breath play
- ❏ Snowballing
- ❏ Edging
- ❏ Orgasm denial
- ❏ Bareback sex
- ❏ Anal sex
- ❏ Rimming
- ❏ Irrumatio
- ❏ Risky/Semi-public
- ❏ Chastity cage
- ❏ Sexy use of tail

And in traditional fashion, way more cumshots and creampies than I could count.

Letters to Satan

CHAPTER 1

A RED-LETTER DAY

Damien

"A-fucking-*nother?*" I bellow, thumping my fist on the desktop as Xalreth nonchalantly drops an envelope onto the polished mahogany. Irrational anger, white-hot and explosive, flares to the surface as I stare at the colorful red and white striped paper, with its stupid holly leaves and—gag me—*hearts.*

"Don't these people know how to *spell?!* S-A-N-T-A!" I pound on the desk between every letter. "It's not that fucking hard, is it? Santa and Satan don't even *sound* the same."

Letters to Satan

"Yes, sir, of course they don't," Xalreth says, bored as he flips through the rest of the mail in his hand, leafing through them as though they're nothing more than annoyances.

Honestly, same.

My hands wave in the air as I glare at the offending letters. "Just like that tomato and to-mah-toe business... completely different."

He freezes, sparing a glance up at me. Gods, those solid black eyes get no less creepy, even after decades of working with him. "I don't think—"

"Yes, yes, we're aware you don't think, Xalreth. Leave it to those with more brain capacity so you don't hurt yourself."

A quiet snort rolls from his throat, muttering something that sounds an awful lot like, "I *know* you aren't including yourself in that assessment." As I open my mouth to argue, he interrupts me by holding up the bunch of envelopes and waving them in my direction. "There are a few actual important letters mixed in with the rest, if you're interested in them."

"More important than lazy little whiney humans begging for presents from a bearded man in a red suit?" I ask, flicking the disgusting candy cane letter away from me until it teeters on the edge of the desk.

"I mean, come *on,* am I right?" My voice turns into a mocking, high-pitched whine, which I feel is terribly accurate for most members of the human species. "Dear *Santa,* I want a new set of golf clubs or world peace or a goddamned BMW so I can look like even more of a douche. Send me a Turbo Twister 9

12

G. Eilsel

dildo because my model 7 is worn out. Wah, wah, fucking *wah.*"

Xalreth's eyebrow arches, but he doesn't look up from the papers in his hand. "You think The Santa is dealing in vibrators these days?" Irritated, my tail twitches and snaps out, flicking him on the back of his hand with enough force to make him yelp and drop the mail, causing him to finally meet my eyes.

"Petulant little shit," I mutter as he tosses me a smirk and leans to pick up the fallen letters. "And no, I don't think The Santa is involved in anything as interesting as vibrators. Probably still making wooden rocking horses and fucking dictionaries, being the insufferable, goody-two-shoes, pot-bellied asshole he is. Or maybe he's crafting a new style of stick to shove up his ass, uptight fuckface with his holier-than-thou attitude. Right *boring,* if you ask me."

"You've never met him," he points out as he drops two letters in front of me, which I glance at and push aside. "This Santa took over a few years ago."

I furrow my brow, trying to think. "How long has it been since the last Santa came to visit?"

"A few decades. You..." He coughs, a *very* sarcastic sound. "...*accidentally* set him on fire."

"Ahh, that's right," I say, a sly grin spreading across my face at the delightful memory. "Purely a misunderstanding. I was merely showing him that the flame retardant on his suit wasn't sufficient."

"Right," Xalreth says, completely dry. "Because summoned Hellfyre from The Lucifer himself is the same as a common chimney fire." I click my tongue

13

Letters to Satan

and give a noncommittal hum, refusing to voice an opinion on that matter.

It's not *my* fault his elves were slacking in their R&D.

I was simply offering a helping hand by revealing his shortcomings... giving him a chance to make some improvements. Much needed ones, judging by the way he lit up like a barrel full of gasoline. It's not like I *knew* he'd lose his eyebrows. Or that he looked like a lumpy, overboiled potato without them.

It was really quite horrifying.

And to think, my requests for compensation for my mental damages were *ignored.*

"We don't know much about this new guy." My gaze darts to the candy-striped letter still teetering on the edge of my desk and I slide it in front of me, tracing my fingers along the edges of the envelope.

"You're right, Xalreth, we don't. This might be the perfect opportunity to change that."

Once again, his black, pupilless eyes flicker up to meet mine. "I recognize that tone... this is the beginning of one of your terrible schemes."

I scoff, dismissing him with a wave of my hand. "My schemes are *incredible*—"

"What about the time you required Hellhounds to be micro-chipped?"

"Not my fault the mutts had an adverse reaction." Mutts... I use the term loosely, since their primary, unshifted forms are six-foot-something hard bodies sculpted straight from a wet dream.

G. Eilsel

Still, a rambunctious crew if you ever saw one.

"An adverse reaction?" he chokes out in a laugh. "That's a hell of a diplomatic way to say they spontaneously *combust*—"

My tail wedges between his lips, cutting off his words as he suddenly gags and shoots a piercing glare in my direction. "Again, a regrettable side effect that couldn't *possibly* have been predicted."

He fists my tail and yanks it away from his mouth, and I wipe it clean on his shirt. "It happened in literally every single test subject—"

"*Completely* unforeseeable!" I raise my voice, narrowing my eyes and daring him to say anything else on the matter.

So, there was a little charred fur?

A couple of minor explosions that resulted in some disgusting cleanup?

It was all in the name of progress, and I'm nothing if not a progressive Lucifer. "The point is, the troublemakers have calmed down since they know they can be tracked."

And since, y'know, the burn wards are still full.

Completely unrelated, I assure you.

Xalreth still glares. "And don't get me started on the curse cloud that *continues* to roam the east side of Hell."

"Oh, that insignificant thing? Nothing more than a minor nuisance. The victims' eyeballs are growing *back*, after all," I argue, irritated that he is making such a giant deal about such puny little nuances.

Letters to Satan

My eyes narrow as I lean forward, and he could win awards with the level of boredom he's displaying. "You're a pain in my ass, Xalreth. What am I paying you for if not to agree with me?"

"You aren't paying me; I sold my soul to the devil, remember?"

"Bah," I bark, swatting him away, "details. You know you love it here with me."

Xalreth's mouth twitches in what might be the start of a grin as he shakes his head. The unspoken truth between us is that we are each other's closest companions, even if we never openly acknowledge it. The nearest thing to friendship in either of our lives. "Yes, sir... of course I do, sir."

"Oh, fuck all the way off," I mutter, glancing at the three letters before me. My fingers drum against the surface before I snatch the red and white striped monstrosity and tap it against the desktop. "Who's my best portal crafter?"

Xalreth taps his chin thoughtfully, a slight frown creasing his forehead. "It was Amon, but he's staying in the human realm now."

"Humans," I mutter, voice rightfully disgusted. "Gods, they're just so... *gross*, soft and smelly and weak with those freaky ass bellybuttons... falling in love and wanting to be..." A visible shudder moves up my spine as I force the word out. "Hap... hap... *happy*."

"After him, Marissa would be your safest bet."

I nod, reclining in my chair and staring past Xalreth with a grin forming on my mouth. "Get Marissa... and Cherise, as well."

As he gives a slight bow, his brow arches in question. "What need do you have for the royal tailor?"

I gesture at my naked torso and lightweight pants. "I can't make a trip to the North Pole wearing this, now, can I?"

"Oh, mercy, this is fucking *marvelous*!" I twirl in front of the mirror, admiring the intricate details of the coat that Cherise crafted. The fur is luxurious, long and thick, gleaming black with an iridescent sheen like an oil slick, while the hood is so large it can cover my eyes and has plenty of space for my horns. The coat hits past my hips, reaching mid-thigh, and has the *perfect* kick pleat in the back for a dramatic spin.

"It is crafted from the highest quality Cerberus fur and enchanted with Pheonix magic. It should keep you very warm, Lucifer, sir."

With a twirl, I add, "And let's not forget how fabulous I look," placing a sassy hand on my hip.

"Oh yes, sir, very fabulous, sir. The *most* fabulous," she agrees, and I narrow my eyes, searching for sarcasm. When she only smiles serenely—as serenely as a demon can, in any case—I nod again.

Letters to Satan

As she explains each piece of clothing she has crafted for me, I run my fingers over the intricate details. There are several pairs of thick, leather-hide pants, a stack of extra-warm sweaters, and a pair of boots with a fur lining so soft, my toes are ready to cream themselves.

"Those give me a toe-boner," I announce, and her eyes immediately widen with nerves.

"I'm... so sorry? Sir?"

I wave her off, glancing over my shoulder at my reflection to see how my ass looks through the kick-pleat. "No, no, it's a good thing... Xalreth!" I shout, and he comes bustling in the door, his solid black eyes wide in the mirror. "Is a toe-boner a good thing?"

"If you have a foot fetish, then I would say definitely, sir."

"See?" I gesture vaguely and Cherise nods like I've given her the wisdom of the gods. Smart one, she is.

"Did you coordinate with the portal maker yet?" I ask, facing Xalreth.

"Yes, Lucifer. Marissa is on standby until you are ready to leave."

"Perfect," I murmur, a wicked grin spreading across my lips as I rub my hands together theatrically. "Have we informed The Santa of our visit?"

Xalreth raises his brows at me as he slowly shakes his head. "No, sir, you strictly forbade me from reaching out to the North Pole to warn them of our arrival. You wanted it to be... how did you word it?" He gives a dramatic pause, thumping his pointer finger on his chin. "Ah, yes... 'The biggest motherfucking surprise of the year.' And when I dutifully asked, 'How big of a surprise is that, sir?' your response was, 'A donkey-dick giant-sized surprise that can be seen from outer space.'"

"That does sound like something I'd say," I agree with a nod.

"Oh, very much, sir." I glare as Xalreth clasps his hands in front of him, suddenly very interested in looking at the imaginary lint on his shirt. When he notices me still staring, he attempts a smile, but his razor-sharp teeth make it more menacing than calm.

"Cherise!" I shout, and she startles since she was only a foot away.

"Yes, my Lucifer?"

"Pack my bags, because Papa's leaving for the North Pole."

"Dear god, don't ever call yourself that again," Xalreth groans, and I reach with my tail to slap him, but he dodges out of the way. "What time should we plan to arrive at The Santa's front door?"

"When would be the biggest inconvenience? Middle of the night? Right at dinnertime like a robo-caller? Five minutes before his alarm clock goes off in the morning?"

"Hmm..." He taps his chin as he thinks. "It's less than a month until Christmas and I bet his workshop is running double-time. Showing up during the workday might cause the most disruption."

Letters to Satan

"Oooh, good call. We'll make a big scene when he shows us around the workshop, too. Distract his minions and get his assembly line all sorts of fucked up."

"I believe they are called 'elves,' sir," Xalreth says, but I dismiss his words with a flick of my hand. I glance in the mirror, catching my wide brown eyes and fluffing my thick blonde curls.

Thought the devil would have dark hair, didn't you?

That's what you get for stereotyping.

"Would sharpening these make me appear more threatening?" I ask, poking at the blood-red horns that stick through my hair. "Like, should it look as though I could disembowel a man just by head-butting him, or is that overkill?"

"Overkill is kind of your schtick," Xalreth says, and well…

I couldn't agree more.

"Cherise!" I shout, and she jumps in surprise again. Poor girl needs to have that anxiety checked out. "Find someone who can sharpen my horns and wax my tail."

"Wax… your… tail?" She glances at the long, leathery, spear-tipped tail, which is the same color as my horns. The rest of my skin is a more muted tone of red, brightest only at my extremities. "It's not… hairy? Sir?"

"Not like *that*." My exasperation is obvious as my hands wave through the air. "I mean, wax it! Make it shiny! Go at it Mr. Miyagi style."

20

Slowly nodding, she edges closer to the door. "Yes, Lucifer, sir. I'll get right on that."

"We should have a royal waxer," I tell Xalreth as I slide my hand over my tail. "In case this becomes a regular thing."

"Yes, a royal waxer," he says, his tone as dry as the desert sun. "That'll be a priority for the next time you want to... polish your tail."

"You don't have to make it sound so perverted."

"Nor do you." I glare at his sass. "Sir," he adds, like the snarky asshole he is.

"Come on, let's go pack."

"*We're* going to pack, Damien?" My side-eye is gentler, knowing he reserves my given name for when we're alone. He's one of the few that's allowed to address me in such a casual way.

"Well, you'll pack, and I'll supervise."

"It's what you do best," he mutters, and this time, he doesn't avoid the swat on his hand.

CHAPTER 2

THE LUCIFER'S (MANY) TITLES

Damien

Marissa takes a step into my private portal chamber, her eyes wide with curiosity and maybe a little fear. Understandable, considering few are permitted into my personal chambers. "Lucifer... your Devilishness, sir," she stammers, her weird attempt at a curtsey falling short and turning awkward.

"I hear you are the best with portals?"

She licks her lips, her gaze shifting between the multiple pieces of luggage Xalreth is juggling, before finally settling on my Cerberus coat. The

G. Eilsel

oppressive heat causes sweat to stream down my spine, but I still push my hip out, savoring her envy.

It is a fabulous coat, really.

"I was at the top of my class for creating portals, and I have been serving the hierarchy for decades."

"Fantastic. I need a portal to the front door of The Santa's workshop." Inside Hell, I'm able to teleport myself anywhere I'd like with just a thought, but travelling outside the realm is quite a bit more complicated.

She nods, her hands fidgeting in front of her. "Yes, sir, Xalreth informed me of your needs, and I am prepared whenever you are ready to travel."

I turn to Xalreth. "Drekoth will run Hell in my absence, and I'm trusting you'll keep in close communication with the Underworld while we're away." Drekoth is my second-in-command, an easy-going incubus that has no desire to attempt a coup on my throne.

Not that he could, of course.

I'm a goddamned force to be reckoned with.

He's a competent leader, just not overly excited to do much of anything. One of the few incubi I've met that won't even work for a booty call. Gods, I bet he is horrid in bed, and a sudden image of him laid out like a sloth, that purple anaconda he calls a dick just hanging out and waiting for someone to jump aboard. The thought makes me shudder.

There's nothing worse than a lazy top.

23

Letters to Satan

Xalreth shoots me a funny look before he responds, "Yes, sir, we will keep a close eye on everything while we're in the North Pole."

I give him another nod. "Marissa!" I bellow, and she jumps clear off the ground.

"Y-y-yes, Lucifer?"

"We're ready."

She nods as Xalreth steps closer, crowding into my side as he repeats his instructions. "Portal us straight to the front door and be on standby for the first few hours in case we have any reason to flee. I will be in touch when we are set to return."

"Yes, sir, I'll be waiting for your orders," she says, holding her hands in front of her as the familiar buzz of magic hums in the air. A minuscule light, barely larger than a match's flame, shimmers and shivers as it builds the path to our destination. Little by little, it grows in size until the blinding white of snow is revealed on the opposite side. It's like looking through a window, except the edges wobble and there's no barrier of glass to stop the chill from blowing through.

A stray piece of snow flutters through, evaporating the very millisecond it hits the fiery atmosphere. More instinct than necessity, Xalreth closes his coat tighter over his broad chest. I give the plain design a once-over, smirking because it's not as fabulous as mine.

"Are you ready?"

"Oh, I was born ready, motherfuckers." Excited to make the North Pole my bitch, I strut towards the portal before his giant hand wraps

G. Eilsel

around my biceps and slingshots me back. "Oh, sweet baby Jeebus!"

Xalreth glowers at me, confusion interrupting his irritation. "Jeebus?"

"Yes, yes, you know... the baby in the goat trough."

"I think you mean... Jesus, sir."

"That's exactly what I said!" I snap, ripping my arm from his grip. "Why did you manhandle me? You know I don't like you like that."

His solid black eyes make it impossible for me to tell if he's rolling them, but intuition tells me he absolutely is. "Let me go first, Dam—" He stops abruptly and glances at Marissa, who is watching our interaction with wide eyes, before composing himself and reverting to a formal tone. "Lucifer, let me go first and ensure it is safe."

"Safe?" I scoff, making a show of rolling my eyes and flipping my hair. "What do you think is going to happen, exactly? I'll trip on an elf? A reindeer will chew my hair?" I puff my chest out, releasing a burst of my power to hang heavily in the small room. "I am the leader of Hell, not a child that needs your protection."

"Regardless, we don't know what to expect, and you are too important to put in unnecessary risk. Allow me the honor of going first, if only for my peace of mind."

Blast him and his gift for words. He knows far too well how to get his way, and I narrow my eyes as I deflate with a dramatic sigh. "You will not act as a

25

Letters to Satan

protector because I don't *need* protection. If anyone is there, you will announce my arrival."

"Announce you, sir?"

"Yes, you can be my master of ceremonies, just like they have in those medieval shows I binge watch." Hello, gluttony. It's my favorite of the seven sins.

"But—"

"Like in Mary, Queen of Scots." Such a fucking wonderful show, especially when the heads start rolling.

"Uh..."

"Oh, and Bridgerton. Can't forget that one."

"That... is ridiculous," he says, putting a saucy hand on his hip. "I will not stand in the snow and shout your titles."

"Hmmm... won't you, though? I bet Jeebus had a badass master of ceremonies," I muse, and his hands fly up in the air. My sigh stretches out long and heavy as his gaze remains fixed on me. "Alright, *fine.* You may go in front of me."

Xalreth appears satisfied as he lifts the armful of luggage once more, ready to take a step towards the portal. I cross my arms and glance at him, juggling the suitcases. "Oh yeah, you're going to be *really* safe with your hands full. What's your plan, to smack an attacker with your toiletries bag?"

He snarls at me over his shoulder. "You could carry your own shit."

"No, no, carry away. I'll just sit here and watch in case the North Pole becomes a bloodbath. That way, if a Yeti tries to eat your head off, I can swoop in to save you, and you'll owe me another life debt." He shakes his head and steps forward, and just like that, he's on the other side of the portal.

His voice is muffled and warbling as it reaches me. "Oh, bastard sons, oh, holy *shit,* it is fucking freezing!" He dances between his feet while trying not to drop my bags.

"Focus! Is there anyone there? Any Yetis?" I shout, and he shakes his head.

"Empty. Come on through." The moment I step through, a stinging cold surrounds me, causing goosebumps to form on my skin. My coat helps against the bite of winter, and the phoenix magic tingles as it works to counter the frigid temperature, but the transition from a triple-digit atmosphere to this severe weather is a shock to my system.

"Jeebus Cracker!" I shout, tucking my freezing hands into my armpits. "What are you standing here for?! Go knock on the door!" My tail dips into the snow, and I'm convinced it's going to freeze right off as I yelp, yanking it up and burrowing it underneath my coat.

Xalreth raises his fist, knuckles facing the door. "Wait!!" I shout, and he jolts and fumbles with one of my suitcases, whirling to glare at me. "Let me just..." I adjust my position, pushing a hip out and fluffing my hair. "Okay, okay, I'm good."

His hand lifts again, arcing towards the door. "WAIT!"

"For fuck's sake, Damien!" he shouts, flinging my bags to the ground and sending a dusting of snow over both of us. I stare at him, unblinking, as I pull

Letters to Satan

out my Chapstick and slowly drag it over my mouth before smacking my lips together. "Are you fucking ready now?"

"Yes." There's a dangerous clip to my voice that has his spine straightening and head tilting in submission. His movements are stiff as he picks up my bags and raises his hand once more. Shooting a quick glance over his shoulder, he waits for my nod before his powerful fist thunders against the door.

From inside, the sound of shuffling is followed by a panicked squeak that makes me grin. Frantic, whispered conversations hiss between at least two voices before the door cracks open. With a head full of wild brown hair and wide blue eyes that seem too big for her face, a rosy-cheeked elf peers through the crack.

"H-hello?" Her petrified gaze bounces back and forth between me and Xalreth, pingponging so fast it almost makes me dizzy.

Xalreth's voice booms so loudly I jump. "Announcing the arrival of The Lucifer, The King of Darkness... The Serpent of Hell, Mighty Legion of the Underworld..."

My brows climb higher on my face with every word, because as loud as he's being, his tone is completely, utterly flat.

This isn't anything like Bridgerton.

"The Ruler of Fire and Brimstone... His Royal Highness of the Infernal Land of the Damned..." As subtly as possible, I kick his shin and he smirks, giving me the quickest side-eye in the world as he clears his throat. "The Devil Himself requests an audience with The Santa."

"The... Santa? The... the *Devil*!?" This tiny person in the doorway sounds like a field mouse when she speaks, squeaking and chirping to where I can barely understand her.

"Yes, elf!" Xalreth bellows, and the face disappears with a frightened peep before reluctantly returning. "His Highness has travelled far to meet with your leader, and we request an immediate audience."

Those giant blue eyes sweep over me, stopping to fixate on my fabulous coat before swallowing with a dramatic gulp. When she speaks again, her voice quivers and her lip trembles. "I'll... just... The Santa is very busy this time of year, but I'll try to... find... him..."

"Are we expected to stand out here in the freezing cold?" I demand, speaking for the first time, and the elf's terror magnifies. She's visibly shaking as she clutches the door, opening and closing her mouth as she tries to form words, but her little elf brain appears to be as frozen as my nuts are going to be if we don't get inside soon.

A rich, rumbling voice comes from behind her, and heavy footsteps approach. "Now, Pattie, we have rules against being rude."

"Y-y-yes, sir, but..."

"No arguments," he says in a firm, gentle tone, while a huge hand inches her to the side. The door swings open and my entire field of vision is replaced by a bright red suit. It's not velvet and fur like I

Letters to Satan

expected, but a form-fitting sweater over a pair of tailored pants.

My chin tilts up to find a chiseled jawline covered with a salt-and-pepper beard, neatly groomed and not a hair out of place, with a broad nose that's tinged pink by the cold. A head full of thick, unruly hair is the same distinguished shade as his beard, and narrowed green eyes study me, wrinkles in the corners displaying laugh lines that stretch almost to his hairline.

He clasps his hands in front of himself and cocks an eyebrow, not speaking. Waiting with an iron will that gives me the impression he'll stand here all day in this silent standoff, refusing to be the first one to speak.

Holy fuck.

Santa is a Daddy.

CHAPTER 3

THE DEVIL AT YOUR DOORSTEP

Niklaus

A commotion unfolding around the front door steals my attention away from my conversation with Cadbury, the head elf. Production for Christmas is tight this year, and I'm afraid we'll only fall further behind if we can't pinpoint the root of the slowdown in our toy department.

"I'm still not convinced that Jujube isn't finding ways to dodge his work... and possibly persuading others to do the same. He's been caught napping in fabric storage more times than I can count." For such a small man, he shoots a rather intimidating glare across the room at the suspect in

Letters to Satan

question, scratching his snow-white beard in suspicion. Jujube, a wiry redheaded elf, has his arms up in a lazy stretch, then scratches his belly like he just woke up.

Maybe there's merit to Cadbury's assumption.

When he catches us studying him, he jumps back to work with a smile that's a bit too forced to be natural. It's borderline manic, and downright creepy.

The increasing commotion at the door returns my focus to it. "Uh huh," I mutter absentmindedly, my eyes fixed on Pattie as she peers through the narrow gap of the massive wooden door. The opening is hardly wide enough for a finger to pass through, and I'm unsure how she can see what lies on the opposite end.

"Apologies, Caddy, we will resume this discussion later." As I pat him on the shoulder and walk towards the door, my confusion intensifies.

"... His Royal Highness of the Infernal Land of the Damned..."

What the...?

Unable to glimpse outside without making my presence known, I wait for just a moment longer while a pompous voice continues, rumbling in a deep growl. "The Devil Himself requests an audience with The Santa." Their conversation creates a whirlwind in my mind as I try to keep up with the back-and-forth.

The Devil is here?

Six years ago, I accepted the role of Santa, but besides the essential supernatural ambassadors needed for the transition, I've met none of the other leaders. Vague stories about my predecessor's visits to the Underworld are confusing at best, with rumors of heated arguments, singed eyebrows, and scorched clothing.

Oh, and something about emotional damage lawsuits? It's never been very... clear.

The Lucifer is more of an urban legend than an actual person... something used to frighten children into eating their vegetables and going to bed on time.

We all know he exists, but he's not tangible. Not *real*.

Not pounding at my door at eleven fifty-three in the morning.

"Are we to stand out here in the freezing cold?" A different voice interrupts my thoughts, this one smoother and not as deep as the first, though with the same level of arrogance.

Despite myself, my interest is piqued.

Gently, I lay my hand on the elf's shoulder, causing her to tense beneath my touch. "Now, Pattie, we have rules against being rude."

Her eyes are wide—wider than normal, that is, which is a feat on its own. Elves have an innate cuteness that serves as a defense mechanism, with their oversized eyes, small button noses, and cheeks that are always perfectly rosy. "Y-y-yes, sir, but..."

"No buts." With a subtle nudge, she yields, allowing me to open the door and reveal two men waiting on the other side. The first is quite large, my height, with pallid, grayish skin and eyes as black as night. He's holding an arm full of...

Letters to Satan

Huh.

Shiny red suitcases with flames stitched into the patent leather.

A little on the nose, I'll admit, but who am I to judge?

The second man clears his throat impatiently, and my head tilts lower as I glance him over. His skin has a soft, rosy hue, and his gorgeous blond curls are swaying in the gentle breeze, sharp ruby horns peeking through the fluffy locks. The intensity in his honey brown eyes is palpable as he narrows them while glaring at me, his scowl perfectly held. My gaze drifts down to his coat that is utterly ridiculous.

I mean, it's downright *tacky.*

"Well?" he finally says, and my eyes snap up to his. "Are you planning to leave Hell's royalty standing outside your door like a mere commoner?"

Feisty little shit.

My grin is barely contained as I tilt my head to one side, taking in the faint maroon freckles that decorate his nose and cheeks. His face scrunches, wrinkling up in a way that's both infuriating and adorable. If this man wasn't such an arrogant asshole, I might describe him as beautiful.

Breathtaking, even.

"Of course not," I finally answer, finding my voice. "Summon your leader and let them know they will be welcomed graciously into our home."

"Su-su-*summon*?!" he stutters, indignant, and a speared tail whips out from underneath the woolly mammoth wrapped around his chest.

G. Eilsel

"Sir," the gray demon interrupts, taking a step forward that makes my body tense. "You will show respect when you speak to The Lucifer and address him by his proper titles." My eyes flare wide as they dart back to the adorable man to his left.

This is the Devil?

This petite, curly-haired, doe-eyed twink on a stick?

Oh, holy sugar cookies.

Those honeyed eyes narrow on mine, and I collect myself with a polite nod. "Please accept my apologies, Your... High... ness?" I hesitate, not knowing which titles to use.

"Lucifer is fine," he says, eyes narrowing even further until they're little slits of irritation.

"Lucifer, then. As you know, I am recently appointed to this role. We haven't yet had the pleasure of being introduced, and I did not recognize you—an unfortunate mistake on my end that will not happen again. You must be a fearless leader to come alone with just one guard."

And they said I couldn't be diplomatic when the situation calls for a gentle hand.

"Fearless, did you hear that? Take notes," he says as he nudges the large demon. Lucifer is pleased as a peacock as he rolls his shoulders, and a smattering of snow falls off the thick black fur of his coat. "Thank you for noticing, Santa. I needed no guards at all, but this one is a worrywart. Perhaps your assessment will make him remember how brave The Devil is."

Letters to Satan

"The bravest, sir," the gray-skinned demon agrees, and I bite at the inside of my cheek to keep from smiling at how Lucifer's narrow chest puffs out in pride.

"Please, come inside out of the cold." I back up and pull the door open, singling out a few elves from the group that have stopped to gawk. "Choco, Plummy, grab their bags so Mister…" I glance at the demon in question.

"Xalreth."

"Bless you."

He stares at me, which is quite unnerving with those inky, bottomless eyes. "My name is Xalreth," he says, with a deliberate slowness, enunciating every syllable.

Well, that's a great start to diplomatic relationships with Hell, telling an ambassador his name sounds like an allergic reaction.

I clear my throat with a hasty, "Apologies," and refocus my attention on the elves hovering nearby. "Please take their luggage so Mister Xalreth doesn't have to carry them everywhere." Timidly, they obey, walking over and accepting the suitcases from the large demon, then glancing at me for further instruction. "Place them in two of the guest suites. If that's okay," I add with a glance in The Lucifer's direction.

"That is acceptable," he says, his freckled nose lifting into the air in a haughty, pompous gesture.

Prince of Hell, indeed. He certainly looks as though he could use someone putting him in his place.

Maybe on his knees.

"Come, gentlemen, let me escort you to my office. I'm assuming there's a reason behind your visit beyond social niceties?" Xalreth nods as The Lucifer glances around, his wide eyes absorbing the bustling activity in the main area of the workshop. Elves are everywhere—hundreds of them, each with a task to do—and it causes quite the disturbance when one of them notices a visitor in our midst.

I cringe as a few of them collide, their feet tangling as they clumsily drop their gifts and toys, creating an explosion of noise. Faces flushed pink and eyes on the floor, the elves gather the items in a rush and hurry away to continue with their tasks. Whispered conversations pass in a buzz of hissing voices, the usual lively chatter dulled as they openly stare.

If failing to recognize Lucifer was the first strike, this was the second, and I'm on the verge of striking out. All eyes fall on me as I clear my throat again, needing to get this game back on track.

"As you were." Immediately, everyone springs into action, although I still notice some staring from the corner of their eyes.

"Yeah, as you were." Lucifer puffs out his chest as he speaks, and I stifle a smile, aware that he wouldn't take kindly to being laughed at. Large elven eyes blink at him before I raise my brow, and they jump back to work.

I decide the only way we're going to make it out of here is if I take charge. "Allow me?" I ask, offering my crooked arm towards Lucifer. Xalreth's

Letters to Satan

gaze sharpens, but I ignore him and focus on Lucifer as he stares briefly at my arm before wrapping his hand around my forearm and clasping. His fingers are brighter than the rest of his skin, a similar ruby to his horns and tail.

We walk through the workshop, and I point out a few areas of interest. Several doors branch off from the main area, each leading to a different specialty section, such as books or clothing, beyond the usual toys and trinkets. "That one's empty," Lucifer points out, gesturing towards a darkened doorway.

"Ah, yes... that was the Furby room for a long stretch in the nineties, then again for a brief run a few years ago. There's no need for it now."

"Furbies are creepy as **FUDGE**." Lucifer's eyes get enormous as he shouts the word. "Oh, dear baby Jeebus, what the **FIDDLESTICKS** just happened?"

A light laugh sneaks out of my throat as he whips his head up to face me. I grin down at him, placing my hand over his, and am surprised as a small jolt passes between his warm skin and mine. "There is magic in the workshops that prevents the elves from cursing, or else it turns... nasty. They're actually quite crude."

His eyes bulge as his mouth sags, and my gaze drops to his pouty, pink lips. "You're telling me I can't curse? What happens if I say **SUGAR COOKIE! SHITAKE!**" He squeezes my arm as Xalreth tries very hard not to react. "Why the **FUNYUNS** does it change every time?!"

"Part of the fun." I offer him a smile, and he cocks his head at me like he can't quite figure me out.

Welcome to the club, buddy.

"You know the man who invented Furbies is in Hell, right? We torture him with his own invention, and don't even tell him when they'll strike. It'll be the middle of the night, and one will go off under his bed." He gives a quick shudder, gripping my arm tighter. "Sometimes days will go by, just to give him a false sense of security, and then, bam! Creepy laugh engaged."

"They are evil little creatures," I agree with another small smile, and he glances back up at me, still with that unreadable expression. My fingers brush lightly over his, my thumb swiping over the back of his hand, and I find I enjoy the feel of him beneath me. His fingers lift to reciprocate my gentle touches, and a spark of something flutters in my chest, but the sneer that Xalreth shoots in my direction makes me withdraw.

Are they lovers?

A small blush burns at my cheeks as I guide them into my office. "Please, make yourselves at home. I'm sure you're still chilled from your time out in the weather, so I'll have Cadbury bring hot chocolates to help you thaw."

Lucifer releases me as he drops into a plush chair across from my desk, slinging his arm over the back and making himself comfortable. "Oh, that sounds fucking delicious!" As soon as the words leave his mouth, realization hits him and he balks, then

Letters to Satan

appears confused. "Why did it not censor me that time?"

I chuckle as I walk around the desk and drop into my seat. "Perks of being the boss. The enchantment doesn't carry into my office or into the living quarters. It only covers the workshop, and even that is just to ensure no one gets distracted."

A devilish grin pulls across Lucifer's lips as he leans forward. "So, I can say whatever I want to say in here?"

"Something tells me you'll say whatever you want to say, whenever you wish to say it, rules be damned," I tease, and his smirk only tugs deeper. The flashy arrogance he wore like a crown at the door has diminished, prompting me to wonder how genuine it really is.

"Excuse me for just a moment." Not wanting to be rude, I send a quick message to Cadbury asking him to deliver drinks before stashing my phone into my desk drawer. My attention refocuses on the men before me, primarily watching The Lucifer as he calmly tracks my movements. I can almost hear the cogs turning in his brain, always in motion.

Anyone in their right mind realizes how sly the Devil can be, and I can't help but question if his soft, pretty facade is part of his deception. Put you at ease, bat those long eyelashes, and next thing you know, you're gutted on the ground. It's a reminder to stay on track and not let my thoughts wander.

"You'll forgive me for cutting to the chase, but what brings The Lucifer to the North Pole?"

40

G. Eilsel

The way his expression changes from contemplative to alert is almost jarring. "Right," he says, reaching into his pocket and pulling out a stack of papers. "I keep getting these letters, and they're meant for you."

Confused, my brows knit as I accept the envelopes and leaf through them. There are around two dozen, just a handful. "This is how many you've received today?"

Appalled, he placed a dramatic hand on his chest, staring at the letter like they might be imbued with the plague. "Dear god, no! These are from the past six months, and they are extremely distracting, as I'm sure you can imagine. They take my time away from far more important tasks."

I glance at him, searching for any hint of humor, convinced that this *must* be a joke, but he has reverted to his usual state of annoyance.

"Um..." I begin, careful to choose my words correctly. "On an average day, we usually get around five hundred letters, but that amount triples during the period from Thanksgiving to Christmas Eve."

Cadbury chooses that moment to enter with a tray full of hot chocolates, and I raise my brow with a small huff of a laugh. He's gone all out. Steam rises from the mugs of cocoa, each topped with fluffy marshmallows and a candy cane leaning against the side, ready for stirring.

"Thank you, Caddy," I say as he places our cups in front of us. I pull mine to my lips and blow over the surface, but Lucifer takes a long swig without even giving it time to cool.

Letters to Satan

"Careful!" I reach for him as he raises a brow in my direction. What was I going to do, exactly? Swat away the offending drink like a knight in red armor? "You'll burn yourself," I add weakly as his eyes light up and he upends his mug, drinking half of it in a single gulp.

"Aww, are you afraid I'll be hurt?" Lucifer purrs as he flutters his eyes at me, those thick lashes curtaining over his chestnut eyes. "That's cute. Don't worry about me, Daddy Christmas. Hell is hot." He pulls the blistering drink back to his mouth and takes another long swig, completely unaffected.

Oh, that's how it's going to be, is it?

"Daddy Christmas, huh?" I ask, trying not to let it show how much I love the sound of that. As his tongue flicks out to clean his lips, I can't help the way I stare.

Simply checking whether it's forked, of course.

It isn't.

Just pink and soft as it darts between his pouty lips.

He hurls me back to reality as he thunks his mug onto the desk and opens his mouth. "Alright, about the problem at hand. How do you intend to handle these letters that keep finding their way to me? I cannot spare any time for such trivial matters."

"There aren't that many, and they *are* addressed to you." Leaning back, I arch an eyebrow at him, puzzled by his inability to simply place the letter in the outbox to be picked up along with his mail. Xalreth growls low under his breath, and I can almost see Lucifer's hair stand up on end in his indignation.

Little fury cat, showing his claws.

"They are obviously not intended for *me*," he shouts, standing as he jabs his finger into the stack of letters. "Who in their right minds would ask *Satan* for a new car unless they want one for their enemies, already rigged to explode? No, this is *your* problem to fix."

He leans forward over my desk, bringing his face perilously close to mine as he taunts me. "And I'm not leaving until *you* handle it." A quiet, indignant laugh leaves me in a rush of air, because I knew he was a brat. It took less than thirty minutes for his true colors to come out to play.

To prove my point, he swats at the stack of letters and sends them scattering into the air to flutter to the ground.

My palms slam onto the desk and I stand, and a fire flares bright in his eyes as he tilts up to look at me. It's the first time he lets me see it—the predator that lies beneath that adorable disguise. The thrill of a challenge burns over his expression, but if he expects me to bow to him, he has another thing coming.

"Your little temper tantrum isn't winning you any favors, Lucifer. Sit. Down." Shock paints his face as his pupils eclipse his eyes, and his tongue flickers out again.

Is that from nerves?

Or excitement?

I wonder if anyone's ever put him in his place.

Letters to Satan

Xalreth charges me with a snarl, but I reach out and grab him, not taking my eyes off Lucifer as I hold him by his neck. "You are in *my* house, in *my* domain, and you will be respectful. Now sit down before I come over there and *make you.*" My voice is low, calm and quiet, but the threat is there, and it hangs heavy in the air.

We're so close our noses are touching, and Xalreth's struggling breath comes in wheezes.

"What will you do?" Lucifer is breathy, his eyes darting around my face.

Oh, this is interesting.

Fascinating, even.

A smirk slowly spreads across my lips as I tilt my head in amusement. "Don't sound so eager to be punished, Your Highness." That tongue moves over his already shining lips again, and I lower my gaze to track the movement before returning to his eyes, molten honey as they lock on mine. "Now, call off your pet and let's have a civil conversation like gentlemen."

"Xalreth, sit."

I release my grip as he sucks in a long inhale, furious as he twirls towards Lucifer. "Damien, you cannot allow—"

"Sit!" he commands, louder this time, not ending our stare-off as Xalreth fumes, dropping into his chair with a gush of air and a lot of grumbling.

"Damien, is it?" I mutter, and his eyes flare as I reach to place a thumb on the small cleft in his chin. It's so innocent, so unassuming. "Be a darling now

G. Eilsel

and take a seat so we can continue this conversation with a better attitude."

"If you're going to call me by my given name, then it's only fair I learn yours."

I chuckle, tilting his face to the side as he lifts his chin, offering his throat. He's submitting, and I don't know that he even realizes what he's done as a shiver courses up my spine. My thumb digs in, watching in fascination as his lips pop apart. "You may call me Niklaus, but only if you behave."

"I can't promise that," he says, a wicked smile digging into his cheeks.

"Oh, I'd expect nothing less from the devil himself."

Letters to Satan

CHAPTER 4

CURSE FILTERS, BLUE PAINT, AND FURBIES

Damien

Xalreth gives me a side-eye full of attitude from the armchair he's sprawled across, but I keep my eyes fixed on the crackling fireplace ahead. Even inside, the temperature difference is surprising, but I relented and finally removed my coat. A small shudder works through my shoulders as I scoot closer to the flames, soaking in the heat.

A loud sigh comes from my cranky companion, and I unsuccessfully try to rein in my temper. "Are you going to fucking say something, or do you just want to stare at me all day? Not that anyone would blame you. If I weren't me, I'd stare at myself for hours too. I'd offer to pose nude for you,

Letters to Satan

but your tiny little brain might implode and then you'd really be useless."

He scoffs and leans forward with his elbows on his knees, pulling his lips between his teeth. It's a familiar gesture, one that inevitably precedes something I don't want to hear. How he does it without maiming himself with those pointy daggers in his mouth is a mystery. "By submitting to him, you gave him the upper hand."

Anger causes my shoulders to stiffen as I fix him with a glare, trying to laser-focus my irritation into tiny little beams to fry his brain a little. Just a little! Eyeball lasers are apparently beyond the scope of my powers, though, so all I can do is fuss. "Mind your fucking tone. I wasn't giving him the upper hand, nor was I *submitting* to him." Not that submitting to Santa Daddy doesn't sound like a good way to spend an evening, but that's neither here nor there. "We are in his domain, *his* world, and we don't know the extent of the power he holds here. If my memory serves me correctly—*and it does*—he easily held you at bay."

He grumbles but can't deny the unexpected show of strength.

"And besides, we aren't here to wage war with the North Pole. It serves no purpose to be at odds with them. We're here to solve a problem... and maybe cause a few while we have some fun."

"Always with the schemes," Xalreth mutters as his lips twitch, a sliver of his irritation fading. "What sort of problems are you thinking, sir?"

G. Eilsel

I grin, standing and pulling an extra sweater over my head before gesturing for him to follow me. "Come on, let's go explore the workshop while Santa Daddy is busy."

"Santa Daddy?" His eyebrow arches so far up on his forehead, I'm surprised it doesn't take flight. I pretend I don't hear him, sliding my feet into my boots and heading to the door. He relents, following me as we weave through the hallways.

Each elf we walk past has eyes as wide as snow globes and scurries to the other end of the hallway, even though we're not causing any trouble. Not yet, at least. Niklaus had responsibilities to attend to and promised we'd regroup soon to discuss the letters. There was no direct restriction to stay in our quarters, so we are not technically breaking any rules by exploring.

It isn't my fault I'm getting restless.

Or that the elves are terrified of me.

Or that Xalreth's smile looks like a prehistoric sea creature.

We finally emerge into the main workshop, and I scan the room, absorbing how, despite the initial pandemonium, there's a synchronized rhythm to the chaos. It's like watching a river rushing past rocks and navigating obstacles, darting this way and that, all while the flow is somehow never interrupted.

Except, instead of water, they are googly-eyed miniature people in too-bright clothes.

The assembly lines are a flurry of activity as elves dart to and from the meticulously labeled

Letters to Satan

rooms. There's storage for fabrics and stuffing, mechanical parts, paints, wood, metal, and tools, and those are the few that are visible from where we stand.

Most of the materials are routed to the lines, where they are sorted into stacks by those at the head of the long tables. Others are carried into specialty rooms, such as the one for bicycles directly in front of us.

Curiosity gets the best of me, and I wander over to peek inside.

A smaller group of elves works on assembling bikes, their tiny hands moving so fast they become blurs. It's fascinating to witness. At one station, two elves are welding a frame, the sparks reflecting off the glass of their protective helmets. Another duo fastens wheels and seats once the metal has hardened and cooled, and a solo worker sprays the finished frame in a vibrant blue behind a drop cloth barrier.

The elf that's painting meets my eyes and gasps, tripping on her feet as she tumbles backward. Blue paint becomes a fountain and showers over everything in a rainstorm, causing the welders to shout. One of them whirls with his flame still burning bright, and a stack of papers ignites, the paint proving to be an affective accelerant as the fire whooshes into an inferno.

It's all very dramatic, and I'm quite disappointed that I didn't even truly earn the reaction, merely standing here.

Such a waste.

"FUNGI!" an elf screams, while another bellows, "Ah, ***SHEETS!***" A weird chorus of squeaky, censored cursing rings out as more eyes dart our direction, and a familiar deep voice booms in the distance. "What is going on out here?"

"FUNKY!" I shout, grabbing Xalreth by the arm and turning to flee. Before we leave, I whip around and narrow my eyes at the gawking elves inside the burning room. "Snitches get their eyeballs ripped out and shoved up their ***ASPS!***"

"That's not the saying," Xalreth unhelpfully adds.

"Oh, shut up! He's headed this way, and he'll be furious if he thinks I'm involved. Quick!" We duck into a storage closet and pull the door closed behind us, panting as we press our ears against it and listen to the insanity outside. Niklaus's bellow of rage makes me cringe, and I hope my threat is enough to keep the little shits from ratting me out.

I twist to look in front of me, meeting the eyes of a group of petrified elves. They're paralyzed, sitting in a circle around a makeshift table littered with playing cards.

"FUG."

Letters to Satan

"What's going on in here?" I ask, putting my hands on my hips and ignoring all the noises coming from the workshop... and there are a *lot* of noises.

"What's going on in *here*? What the heck is going on out *there*?"

Amused, I tilt my head as a small smile spreads over my face, walking over to stand beside the mouthy elf. He doesn't even flinch, just narrows his eyes at me as I flop onto a pile of fabric. "You're either very brave or very dumb, shorty... or perhaps a touch of each, and that's a dangerous combination. What's your name?"

"Why, you gonna turn me in?" The suspicious glint in his gaze makes me smile wider and I shake my head.

"Turn you in? Of course not, my friend... I'm literally The Devil. You think I give two **SHIPS** about people slacking off at work?" I grimace as my voice carries.

"You've been known to torture people for it in Hell," Xalreth points out, but I dismiss him with a wave.

"That's different because they're my workers." My eyes drift over the other three, who are all fixated on the table. They aren't nearly as stupid as the one beside me with flame-red hair, which makes them far less interesting. "You're obviously the ringleader of this little slack-off group. You may call me Lucifer, and this is Xalreth."

"Bless you," the elf says, and I throw my head back in a delighted laugh as Xalreth growls.

52

"That's my name." He bears his sharp teeth, which causes the other three to shake with such violence I'm convinced they're going to hit the ground like a bunch of bowling pins. It's a stark contrast to my new idiot friend, who looks wholly unbothered when faced down by a razor-toothed demon five times his size.

I've decided I like this guy.

"If you won't tell me, I'll just call you Poddy."

"Poddy?" he asks, full of skepticism.

I shrug. "Squatty Poddy."

One of the others snorts a laugh, then quickly stifles it. "Name's Jujube," he finally says, sticking his tiny hand out in my direction. Grinning, I shake it, then gesture for him to deal me into their game.

"Alright, Jujube, lay it on me. I want all the dirty little secrets and juicy gossip from the North Pole. Is there a squashed lawsuit for poor working conditions? Denied vacation times and unpaid overtime? Does Santa have a rotating door of tiny prostitutes that please him with their itty-bitty mouths?"

That suspicion doubles as he arches a brow at me. "You're not trying to get me in trouble?"

"On the contrary, my friend. I'm looking to get into trouble *with* you."

Jujube considers this for a second, running his fingers through his messy hair. "It's a pretty drama-free environment, honestly. I mean, we're kind of obligated, you know? Where else are a bunch of mythical three-foot-tall beings going to go live and work in peace? Aside from some niche porn or the

Letters to Satan

occasional fairy tale movie role, there's not a lot of demand for us. Hours are standard, and our apartments are provided as part of the gig."

Well, this is boring.

"How about The Santa? What dirt do you have on him?"

"He works us hard and is not overly social. Much stricter than his predecessor, that's for sure, and none of us know him too well on a personal level aside from Cadbury, but I wouldn't call him unfair. It's obvious he cares about those that work for him."

"Any filthy skeletons in his closet? Scorned lovers or fun kinks that got leaked? Tales of spinning naughty elves on his dick like a basketball?"

"Uh, no, dude, not that I've heard. Boss man keeps his personal life private."

I wave my hand around the room, gesturing at the secretive card game. "So, if the work conditions are good and Santa's not some creepy bearded perv, why are you in here playing poker instead of doing your job?"

Jujube looks at me as though I have two heads as he rolls his eyes. He's a ballsy little shit, I'll give him that. "Because we're lazy. Being an elf doesn't mean we hum and sing while we go about our day."

"You don't all whistle while you work?"

"That's dwarves, assho—"

Watching Xalreth slam the snarky elf against the wall fills me with glee that amplifies when I hear the terrified squeak that follows. Xalreth's black eyes narrow as Jujube looks like he might have a heart attack, tiny feet dangling in the air. "The Lucifer will

54

G. Eilsel

not be disrespected in my presence, twerp. Do we have an understanding?"

"Yes!" It's more of a strangled chirp than actual words, but the meaning is clear. Xalreth releases him and he crumples to the ground, holding his neck and wheezing.

"Anyway!" I say cheerfully as I play my next card, and Jujube cautiously returns to his seat beside me. "I had an idea for something… fun… if you're interested."

"Oh?" His voice is raspy, but he can't hide his curiosity.

"How hard would it be to wrangle a few more helpers and gain access to that unused Furby room?" There's a familiar glint in his eyes that tells me he was the right person to ask.

CHAPTER 5

Niklaus

Fuming, I storm into my office, taking a few deep breaths in an attempt to quell the anger roiling under my skin. Whoever started the rumor that Santa was patient and jolly was fucking *wrong*, because I need blood pressure medicine and a heavy drink after today.

When I went to check on progress in the workshop, I found it in absolute anarchy, stemming from the bicycle room. Paint coated every surface inside, fire was chewing up everything flammable, and the elves were terrified.

G. Eilsel

Not a single one of them could provide an explanation, as they all seemed to experience a mysterious case of temporary amnesia. They remembered every other detail, down to the last time the paint sprayer was reloaded, but anything involving the mess?

Nada.

They were locked up tight. Only after things had calmed down and I spoke to them one-on-one did Brie let a single word slip.

"Lucifer."

Once she whispered it, her lips were glued shut once again, and she refused to say anything else. Now, I'm no idiot. You invite the Devil into your home and it's a guaranteed recipe for disaster. I'd be remiss not to believe her.

There's just one problem.

Damien was nowhere to be found near the scene of the crime.

Not sneaking through the workshop or cackling in the corner. He didn't stand there smiling at the chaos he'd created. No, there wasn't so much as a hint of his pointy horns or twitchy little tail, and I hung around, waiting to see if he would crawl out of a hole somewhere.

I was ready to blame him. Prepared to banish him from this place, send him back into Hell where he belongs, but he just... wasn't there.

Furiously, I yank off my thick red sweater, the neon blue streaks and lingering smoky odor a glaring reminder that I still have no idea what happened. Right as I toss it aside, there's a knock on the door.

Letters to Satan

"Yeah, come in," I shout as I walk over to my closet to grab a clean shirt.

Speaking of the devil…

Damien walks in, head tilted in a very cat-like way, his eyes flickering down my torso and snagging on my chest as I pull on my sweater. Only once I'm covered does he meet my gaze once more. His honey brown eyes are concerned and full of innocence as he asks, "What happened to you?"

"A bit of a disaster in the workshop, I'm afraid. You wouldn't happen to know anything about that…" I take a step closer and his narrow chin tilts to peer up at me. "Would you?"

"Who, me?" His heavy blonde lashes flutter in the fakest act of naïveté I've ever seen, but I have no proof of his involvement. Baseless accusations against the Devil would be a foolish and dangerous mistake.

Even if he's currently playing coy.

"I've been in my quarters, warming up by the fire. It is so much colder here than it is in Hell, and it's taking me a while to adjust."

"I suppose that is quite the change."

He takes a half step forward into my space, and I hate how my body is instantly drawn to his. I imagine that the opening page of *An Idiot's Guide to Living* would strongly advise against getting entangled with your enemies, but tell that to my dick. "You could've come and visited me in my quarters, you know. I would've welcomed your…" He glances up at me from under his lashes. "… company."

Gods, the way he says it is almost a purr. "Too bad I was stuck putting out fires."

Literally.

"That is a shame," he agrees, reaching up and fingering the edge of the sweater I just pulled on. "This looks so cozy. I wasn't sure what to pack, seeing as I've never had to brave the cold."

"When's the last time you saw snow?"

His fingers continue to glide over my shirt as his eyes roll up in thought. "Honestly, I couldn't tell you. The previous Santa came to visit in Hell, although I was part of an emissary to the North Pole in my youth before I took over the position."

"How long have you been The Lucifer?" I ask, curiosity piqued, since he doesn't look a day older than twenty-five.

"Trying to learn my secrets, Niklaus?" His fingers swipe under my sweater, barely brushing against my skin, and the heat of his body has goosebumps rising on my stomach. A ball of tension builds and shoots lower, my cock giving a content little twitch.

"Only the ones you're willing to share." He lets out a pleased hum as he releases my shirt and takes a step back, and I gesture at the chair across from my desk.

Blonde curls cascade over his forehead as he sinks into the seat. "I've been in office for one hundred and seventy-nine years."

"And just exactly how old are you?"

Letters to Satan

He grins, flashing me his rows of pearly white teeth. "Now, now, that's not a question you normally ask a gentleman, is it?"

"Are you, though?" I ask, hiking a brow as he leans forward, tilting his head. "A gentleman?"

Another of those infuriating hums leaves his throat before he smiles again, and I'm struck once more by how stunning he is. "When I want to be, I suppose. What about you?" I wave my hand for him to clarify. "How old are you, Nik?"

My lips twitch at the nickname, loving the sound of it coming from him. "Forty-seven," I answer, and he appears genuinely shocked for the first time since we've met. "You're surprised."

"I assumed you were older. Or does the Santa's magic not work like that?"

It's my turn to give one of those noncommittal hums, and I love the way it makes him squirm. "No, it does," I finally say. "The position of The Santa grants long life to the holder."

"How long of a life?"

"Long enough," I answer, and he gets another faint, sly smile on his face when he realizes he's not the only one playing this game of chess. "Now, I've got a few minutes if you wanted to discuss your issue further."

His brows give the tiniest confused flex before realization smoothes them back out. "The letters?"

"Unless there are other issues I don't know about?" Amused humor dances in his eyes as they flicker up to mine, suggesting there is an entire world of secrets hidden behind that charming smile. It's yet another reminder to keep my guard up while he's here.

"Issues? Oh, no," he muses, still with silent laughter painted on his face, and I track him as he stands from his seat and walks to my side of the desk. I spin in my chair to face him, hand on my chin as I watch. "There's probably very little that happens here that you don't know about, I imagine."

"Mmm," I hum, refusing to answer while he's speaking in riddles. I straighten my back as he confidently steps forward between my knees, a small smile gracing his lips before he turns to the side and lowers himself onto one of my legs.

My voice is huskier than I intend as I murmur, "What are you doing?" and he flashes another of those innocent smiles.

"It's how this works, isn't it? You sit on Santa's lap when you tell him what you want."

Years of self-control are tested as he wiggles, and I force myself not to react as my cock flexes, my fingers digging into the arms of my chair until the leather pits. Although I want nothing more, I fight the urge to put this insolent man in his place.

Speared on my cock and bent over my desk, pants around his ankles.

Yeah, that sounds right.

"And what do you want, Damien?"

"Well..." He drags his finger across the line of my jaw before he turns to face the desk, rubbing that pert ass all over my lap. My hand is halfway to gripping his hip when he says, "The issue seems to stem from the supernatural delivery system."

Letters to Satan

I blink a few times, realizing he's actually talking about the mail.

Instead of letting my hand fall, I reach around him and let it rest on his thigh, leaning forward to glance over his shoulder at the stack of letters on the desk. "Well, to be fair, they are seeing *Satan* clearly written on the envelopes. They really can't be blamed for sending them to the intended recipient."

He scoffs, refusing my logic. "They should realize anything with... candy stripes and, and... *hearts* would not be coming to me."

"What is the other option, then? Would you rather the letters be opened before delivered?"

Horror flashes across his face. "Absolutely not!"

"Why not, Damien?" I ask, teasing my fingers over his thigh. "What sort of letters are you getting that you'd be so afraid of others reading? Weekly deliveries from World of Porn?"

Despite his best efforts, he can't conceal the grin trying to overtake his lips. "Don't judge me when I'm ordering holiday specials for the occasion. 'Tits a Wonderful Life' and 'I'll Be Homo For Christmas,' and my personal favorite..."

"Oh, I can't wait to hear this," I mutter.

"Ho ho ho, Santa's Gonna Blow."

I snort a laugh and he lets his grin spread, shoulders shaking as he laughs with me. "Are those classics by Charles *Dick*ens?"

He whirls to face me, a thrilled expression on his face as my hand tenses on his leg. "Look at that! He jokes... he *actually* jokes."

G. Eilsel

"I'll have you know I'm hilarious when I choose to be."

"You just never choose to be?"

"Insolent little shit," I mutter, and his smile twists to a smirk as my fingers drift up his spine, stopping at the nape of his neck. "Has anyone ever put you in your place?"

"Oh, please, like they could tame me." His chin tilts up in an obvious challenge, and my tongue slides between my lips as his eyes dart to watch. "But I'd *love* to see you try."

His hand presses against my chest as he leans in, his face so close I could count the constellation of maroon freckles that speckle his cheeks. Breath dancing over my lips, he freezes just a millimeter away, and my inhibitions disappear when his eyes flutter closed. My fingers flex around his neck as I draw him in, and then a sudden, booming knock causes us to pop apart.

Xalreth charges into my office, furious as he stares at Damien perched on my lap. "What the fuck is going on in here?" he bellows. Cadbury is directly behind him with wide eyes, like he followed him with absolutely no clue how to intervene.

My back straightens as I sit taller, but Damien remains lazily slouched against me as I narrow my eyes. "Not that it is any of your business, *demon,* but we were brainstorming this issue with the mail."

His lip pulls into a sneer, gesturing at the highly inappropriate way we're cozied up in my chair. I tighten my grip on the back of Damien's neck, my fingers grazing the sensitive spot behind his ear,

63

Letters to Satan

and Xalreth's snarl rips up further as Damien tilts his head up, exposing his throat to me.

A tiny smirk plays on my lips at the show of jealousy, wondering what he'd do if I dragged my tongue up that slender neck while he watched. "Would you like to join us for this conversation, Xalreth? I'm sure you'd have some very helpful input."

For a few tense seconds, he fumes in the doorway, before he wipes away his frustration and enters the room. Poised and in control, he smooths his hands over his pants and takes a seat opposite me. His eerie black eyes stay fixed on Damien. "Care to join me, *sir*?" He emphasizes the last word, glaring at his leader.

Damien stills in my lap and my fingers tense around his neck as I inch forward. "You may go sit," I murmur in his ear, and he shivers against my touch before swallowing and rising from his perch on top of me. He takes a seat next to Xalreth, who hasn't blinked once during our interaction.

My smile is more of a baring of my teeth as I lean on my elbows. "Now, gentlemen, where were we?"

G. Eilsel

CHAPTER 6

COME ALONG FOR THE RIDE

Damien

"What are we doing here, and why do we have to whisper?" Jujube asks, crossing his arms over his narrow chest as he hikes a brow at me. Unlike the other elves, he doesn't shy away from maintaining eye contact with me. They're terrified while he's bored.

He must be half demon, I've decided.

I gesture around at the empty production room we're standing in. The lights are off, making it hard to distinguish the faces of those gathered here. It increases the risk of a spy, or someone changing

G. Eilsel

their mind and running to tattle, but it can't be helped.

Aside from myself, Xalreth, and Jujube, there's a small grouping of elves who Jujube swears can be trusted to keep our secret. "We're whispering because if Nik—" Xalreth's black glare darts to me with a sneer, and I roll my eyes but rephrase. "If The Santa finds us here, he's going to be **PIZZAZZED**." The elves giggle and I narrow my eyes until they are quiet. "Unless we can use magic to shield this room from light and noise, we'll have to work quietly in the dark."

A particularly small female elf with blonde hair raises her hand from the rear of the group. I nod in her direction, and she clears her throat before speaking in her squeaky, high-pitched voice. "There are magical workers that could cast a dampening spell on the room, Mister Lucifer, sir."

That has definitely caught my attention. "Intriguing... go on."

"Well, er... it wouldn't eliminate light and sound, but it would dampen it enough that during a normal day in the workshop, I don't think anyone would notice."

I nod again, rubbing my chin as I consider the option. "And do you know someone willing to cast such enchantments... discreetly?"

She hesitates, but Jujube butts into the conversation. "There's a guy in the magic department that owes me a favor."

"Enough of a favor to keep this a secret from The Santa?"

Letters to Satan

His grin is impish, even with his rosy cheeks and upturned nose. "Let's just say that I caught him doing some particularly naughty things inside The Santa's office one night when he was supposed to be refreshing enchantments. The receiving end of these naughty things *also* works in the magic department, so I've got double the resources."

"Fantastic," I say, clapping my hands in front of me, "make it happen. Now, moving onto supplies and tools. We will need a few molds crafted, a heating element and protective gear, silicone in any color you can think of, minor electrical supplies..."

"Decorative gems?" Xalreth suggests from beside me, and my grin spreads.

"Yes, most definitely some decorative gems. We'll make the best butt bling there is."

"Butt... bling, sir?" A mousy elf with squinty eyes hiding underneath half-moon glasses asks, and I turn my wide smile towards him.

"What did you think we were going to be creating in here, toy soldiers? We'll be making toys, alright, my friends, but not the kind you're used to. If you want out, now's the time to leave, otherwise you are officially indoctrinated into my army."

"Army?" Jujube asks, a sly smirk on his face.

"My Army of Hellves."

G. Eilsel

Hours later, I peek out of the workshop door. Magic has been cast, equipment and supplies loaded into their appropriate places, and molds have been designed. Most importantly, the locks have been re-keyed and sealed with a privacy enchantment so that no one aside from me, Xalreth, or the Hellves can unlock it.

I hope.

Unsure of how powerful Santa's magic is in his domain, I'm erring on the side of caution.

My eyes sweep across the workshop, seeing nothing of concern above the sea of heads. The elves are so hard at work, none of them pay me any attention as I slide out of the room and casually close the door behind me with a click, tucking the key into my pocket.

A timid ebony-haired elf works diligently on what appears to be a dollhouse, and I slink over on quiet feet, leaning in until my face is beside her ear. "Ooooh, whatcha making?" I ask, and she releases a blood-curdling shriek, flinging her miniature hammer into the air.

It's mesmerizing, spinning in a few weightless loops before crashing back down, thunking square between the eyes of the elf across the table. "Ouch," I

Letters to Satan

hiss as he groans, eyes rolling up into his head. His tiny body deadweights and crumbles to the ground, knocking the chair out from underneath the elf behind him.

One by one, they fall, squealing like piglets as they hit the floor. It's like a row of wiggly, squeaky dominos falling, one after the other, as the pandemonium spreads along the aisle.

I'm so fascinated I forget to laugh.

"What is going—" Niklaus's deep voice booms through the workshop, his eyes instantly locking on mine. "Lucifer. I should've known you were involved."

My hands fly up, palms facing him. "I was only complimenting the craftsmanship of this dollhouse. It's not *my fault* she is startled so easily."

Niklaus comes closer, his eyes narrowed and suspicious. "Lolli, can you please tell me what happened?"

She's a nervous thing, wringing her hands in front of her as she stares at the floor. "I'm sorry, Santa, sir... he... he's telling the truth. He asked what I was making, and I... I just overreacted."

"Understatement," I grumble, but am ignored.

Niklaus's brow lifts in a very skeptical arch. "That's all he said?"

"Yes, sir. I-I didn't mean to... make such a mess..."

Niklaus puts a soft hand on her shoulder, kneeling in front of her. "It's alright, Lolli. Having guests here is new, and it's natural that you'd be startled by someone you don't recognize." She

G. Eilsel

glances up to meet his gaze, and I realize with horror that she's *crying.* Giant, fat tears pool precariously as she nods, her weak little chin trembling.

"Oh, ew," I mutter, unable to help myself.

Niklaus's eyes carve into mine, a fierce flame flickering behind that emerald stare, filled with a passion that thrills me to my very core. Excitement burns in my gut as I hold the breath in my lungs, desperate to see that temper unleashed.

Slowly rising to his full height, he closes in on me until there's barely more than a few inches separating us. The tension is so dense, I swear sparks crackle and buzz over my skin.

Thick fingers grip my jaw and tilt it upwards until I'm staring into his eyes. "Would you care to join me for a stroll, Lucifer?" he asks, his thumb tugging at my chin until my lips pop apart.

I blink in surprise.

Where's the anger... the boiling temper I was ready to drown in?

He takes a half step backward and offers me his arm, the picture of serenity. My hand loops through the crook of his elbow, gripping on to his thick forearm as I try to figure out what game he's playing.

Elves openly stare as we wander through the midst of their workspaces, Niklaus as calm as can be. "Why is it," he mutters, leaning closer so no one else hears, "that any time something happens, you're always there?"

"Why, I can't say I know what you mean."

"First the bicycle room and now this."

Letters to Satan

Sneaky thing.

It's entertaining how he tries to trap me in a lie while keeping his demeanor so impressively nonchalant. Santa has a few tricks up his sleeve, it would seem. A drawn-out, curious sound leaves my throat as I tap my chin. "Bicycle... bicycle... oh, yes, how could I forget? That was the unfortunate accident that got you all hot and naked in front of me yesterday, correct? While I did rather enjoy the show, I'm afraid I wasn't there for that one."

Not where he could see me, in any case.

He grunts an unconvinced hum, and I'm absolutely thrilled at this little game of cat and mouse. "And the mess just now was nothing more than a misunderstanding, huh?"

"Luck of the draw, I suppose." He smirks at my answer as he leads me through a hallway I have yet to explore. The crowd dissipates until it's only us, surrounded by the soft hum of conversations echoing from the workshop.

"Never thought of the Devil as being particularly lucky," he muses, pushing into a large wooden door. Bright sunlight reflects off the snow outside and temporarily blinds me as we step into the freezing afternoon.

I shiver at the unexpected cold, then twist up to face him. "Why is that?"

He shrugs, staring off into the distance. "Children are frequently warned about Hell through stories. It's supposed to be a dreadful place, full of pain and suffering."

72

"Run by an evil leader who would not hesitate to end their lives as they sleep, am I right?"

His laugh is nothing more than a huff of air through his nose, and he places his hand over mine and squeezes. "Perhaps."

"That's a bit judgmental," I mutter, and he finally glances down at me with a rueful grin. "Hell is not a terrible place to live. Are demons sometimes… rambunctious? Absolutely. However, I'd argue the things that tarnish Hell's reputation are circumstances that are completely out of our hands. Even I have my limitations, you know."

His apprehension has turned to curiosity as he watches me. "I can't believe you admitted that."

I turn my head, so he doesn't catch my grin and how easily it falls into place when I'm with him. "Everyone wants to judge our landscape of fire and brimstone, but how's that extremity any different from your snow and freezing cold up here?"

Niklaus hums, a thoughtful expression on his face. "I suppose I see your point."

"Our moral compass might not be as aligned as other creatures, but most demons are no different from anyone else. They're trying to make a life for themselves with as much happiness as possible. Add in the little tidbit of having to deal with the damned souls of wicked humans, and it adds some stress to the population. Evil souls are admittedly a buzzkill."

"Oh, I imagine they would be."

"But what is the alternative, Nik? Who else is going to bear that burden? Holding those souls is an

Letters to Satan

important part of the balance, and we all recognize that, even if it makes us a bit... testy."

"Interesting word choice," he says, and I grin again. We reach an enormous wooden barn, and he twists to face me. The weight of his full attention lands on me, and I can't help my shiver. "And you?"

"What about me?"

"What happiness are you finding for yourself in life?"

The smirk on my lips falters at his question, but I quickly push it back into place. "Ruling is a full-time gig, as I'm sure you know. Endless responsibilities and never enough time to get them handled. Everyone has an opinion, and they all want to share it. Spare time to gallivant around, trying to find my happiness... well, that's a luxury I don't have, Nik."

His head tilts as he steps into my space, and my back lands against the side of the barn. "You aren't happy?"

"I never said that. There are just too few hours in the day for me to run in circles chasing silly concepts of happiness and love."

"Oh, we're discussing love now, huh?" he murmurs, voice deep, and my eyes dart up to his. There's a swoop low in my belly, and the fluttering that rises into my chest almost makes me dizzy.

It's foreign, and I hate it as much as I crave more.

His forearm rests against the wall above my head, and he leans closer. "The Devil has a heart hidden in that sassy little frame, after all. Tell me, do you cover it up with all that sarcasm because you're afraid others will realize it? Or are you scared to admit it to yourself?"

"I'm not scared of anything," I snarl, and he only laughs, close enough that his warm breath blows over my face.

"Such an insolent thing," he murmurs, licking his lips before he inches closer, eyes locked on mine. "You know what I think?"

"I bet you're going to tell me."

His hand creeps up my arm and gently encircles my neck, and I can't help it as I lift my chin and expose myself to him. It's the ultimate display of vulnerability, and the opposite of what my instincts urge me to do. They want me to reveal my strength, push my power on him, and make him bow at my feet.

But I don't.

Instead, I stand here, throat exposed and pulse pounding against the pad of his thumb.

Somehow, it feels right.

His bottom lip is caught between his teeth as a sultry smile tugs at the corners of his mouth.

"I think you are *dying* to give up that control. You're exhausted from being the one in charge and crave someone else taking the burden of choice from you. You want to be bent until you submit, and you..." Niklaus leans in until his lips brush over mine, and a heavy, choppy exhale blows out of my nose. "You want to obey... and I want to *make you.*"

My mouth drops open, ready to protest, to tell him to fuck off and bring him to his knees. Show him

Letters to Satan

he's not the only apex predator here and prove to him just how much power I hold inside.

Instead, all I do is stare, my eyes darting between his.

"Tell me I'm wrong." His green eyes are ignited as he maintains this tiny gap between us, mere inches separating us and refusing to come any closer. "Tell me you don't feel this, too." There's a certain desperation behind his words as he shakes his head, his lips brushing over mine again with the motion.

"And if I didn't?" I manage, my voice only an exhale. "If I felt nothing?"

"Then I'd walk away, and we'd never discuss this. We would sit down and solve this problem in an hour instead of using this silly procrastination as an excuse. Do *not* deny it," he snarls when I open my mouth to argue. "We're both doing it. I'm allowing chaos to reign in my workshop, watching my deadlines slip further behind as I indulge in this game with you."

"I don't play games."

"Don't you?" I struggle against his palm, pushing toward him until my breathing turns raspy, but he counters me and pulls away, eyes glued to mine. "I should want to throttle you, to send you back to Hell where you came from, and instead, you are *consuming* my thoughts, Damien."

And I want to admit that I'm consumed by him as well, but my mouth refuses to form the words.

It's safer this way, isn't it?

76

The world hates me... it's just a matter of time before he realizes he hates me, too. Happiness isn't for the likes of me. Mischief and chaos, yes, but not joy.

Certainly not *him*.

His chest rises in deep breaths as his nose nuzzles against mine, both of us unblinking. The seconds tick away in silence before disappointment flashes over his eyes, quickly replaced by a hardness that cracks right through my resolve.

"Very well," he says, and I track the movement of his Adam's apple as it bobs in his throat. He moves a half step back, his palm sliding from my neck, and I miss the heat immediately.

Niklaus turns and takes a long stride away, and it's all I can take. "Wait," I rasp, lunging forward to grab his hand, and the full weight of his body slams against mine as he pins me against the barn once more.

"Wait, what?" His voice is so low that it barely rises above a rumble in his throat. "What do you want, Damien?"

My tongue drags between my lips as my eyes dart around his face. He's not letting me out of this, refusing to move a muscle as he waits. "I want you to kiss me," I finally say, jutting my chin out in a final act of defiance.

He clicks his tongue, dragging his thumb over my jawline. "Then ask for it."

My nostrils flare in a heavy exhale as his green eyes bore into mine, his grip on me bruising. "Kiss me, Nik."

Letters to Satan

"Sir."

I toss my head in a barely there shake as I blink at him. "What?"

The very corner of his lip pulls up in a small smirk, pitting the skin there into a dimple. "Kiss me, *sir*. Say it."

A quiet scoff rolls from my chest as my brows bunch, but he only watches me with that maddening thumb swiping over my chin, just below my lip. He leans in, and for a moment, I think he's going to give me what I want, but he bypasses my mouth and puts his lips against my ear. "It's up to you to ask for what you want."

Another rough swallow works my throat as he backs up, hooded eyes on mine as he hovers directly in front of me.

Wanting.

Waiting.

"Kiss me, sir," I finally whisper, and this time, both sides of his mouth tip up in a smile. "Please?"

"That's better, now, isn't it?" he murmurs, and his lips crash into mine.

The unexpected scrape of his beard against my chin causes me to gasp, but the surprise burns into the need to match his every move. The confident, slow dance of his lips makes me feel like I'm melting into him, like he's siphoning the free will from my body.

There's no questioning who's in control as he slides his hand back up my chest, gripping my chin and positioning me where he wants me. And as much as I thought I'd fight it, I find myself willingly surrendering.

He kisses me until my lips tingle, until the pressure of his mouth and the rasp of his facial hair make them swell, and then he scrapes his teeth over my bottom lip and drags my mouth open. His tongue pushes its way inside, and I'm helpless to do anything but just hold on as he ravages me.

My hands drag up his arms and reach around his neck, a shiver working up my spine at the low growl that forms in the back of his throat. In one smooth motion, he kicks my foot and spreads my legs. He wedges his leg between mine, his thick thigh against my crotch, and my hips jut forward, completely out of my control.

"Oh, you like that, do you?" he murmurs as he moves one of his hands to my ass, rocking my aching cock along his leg.

"Fuck, yes," I moan as I tuck my face into his neck, unabashedly grinding against him as his fingers edge closer to the crease of my ass. They tiptoe closer and closer, and his chilly thumb hooks under my waistband.

His hand travels up my back until his palm is flat against my spine. "Yes, what?" he asks, slipping into my pants. His middle finger glides down until he's inches away from my hole, and I'm burning alive as I thrust against him.

He freezes, and I twist my body, desperate for contact. "Yes, *what*?" he repeats, infuriatingly still.

"Yes, Daddy, I like that," I gasp, and his low, husky chuckle is in my ear. "I really fucking like that."

Letters to Satan

"Daddy, huh?" he murmurs, and his hand slips further until his fingertip pushes on my hole. The shock of cold only makes it better as he pulses his finger, claiming my lips in a rough, hurried kiss. He presses his weight into me, the swell of his cock behind his pants jabbing into my stomach. "You want Daddy to take care of you, is that it? That's what the Devil wants? To be treated like a prince?"

"Yes," I gasp as he rubs my asshole, teasingly slow as he rolls his hips, perfectly in control even as he unravels me altogether. "Tell me what you'll do to me, Nik... how you'll ruin me."

"Eager thing," he mutters as he nips at my lip. "I'll fuck the cocky attitude right out of you, Damien. Bend you over my desk with your hands pinned so you can't touch yourself, and it won't be soft and sweet, little prince. That's not the way you want to be pampered, is it? You'd rather have it hard and rough, and that's what you'll get. You'll moan like the little slut you are while that tight ass squeezes around me."

His thick finger slips inside me, and my hole clenches as I gasp. He works it deeper as I grind against his thigh, my head thunking against the barn wall as my breath comes out in white puffs of steam. "Please, Daddy, please," I whisper, turning it into a chant as I lose control of myself.

He thrusts into me until he's knuckle deep, and then he starts to stretch a second inside. There's no lube, not even a courtesy spit, and it burns as he works it in. My cock aches, and my balls draw tight as I whimper and wail, the sting sending me floating

G. Eilsel

high off the ground. "Please," I whine, "please, please…"

That second finger slips past my rim, and I gasp as lightning-fast, unexpected pleasure crashes over me, clouding my vision and ringing in my ears. My cock thumps inside my pants as hot cum soaks into the fabric, and my hole pulses around his fingers. Throaty, desperate moans slice through the silence as I thrust against his leg, a warm dampness spreading over my crotch and stamping against his jeans.

"What a good boy, coming in your pants for me," he murmurs, still fucking me with his fingers as I float through the waves of pleasure. "Didn't even have to touch your cock, did you? Are you a little pillow prince that just sits back and lets Daddy do all the work?" I nod, and he chuckles, slipping his fingers from my ass before he drops to his knees, pinning me in place with his palms on my hipbones.

"Do you want me to clean you up, too?"

Oh, dear *God*, this man.

"Yes, Daddy," I whisper. With a low, pleased hum, he leans forward and wraps his lips around my half-softened dick under my pants, giving a gentle suck that makes me jerk my hips. His tongue slips out, dragging over the fabric and teasing me as I whimper, thickening under the heat of his mouth.

"That's a good little prince," he murmurs as he unzips me and pulls my cock out, licking over the head and groaning at the taste.

Both of us freeze at a noise in the distance, and two distinct, familiar voices go back and forth.

Letters to Satan

Nik curses and stands, tucking me into my pants, then staring at my soaked crotch. He yanks his sweater off and tugs it over my head, surrounding me with his warm, spicy scent. It's huge, hitting past my thighs and hiding what we've done.

There's just one problem now.

Him.

Shirtless, he looks like a goddamned snack with that broad chest exposed and nipples pebbled against the cold. His thick cock pushes against his jeans, and his knees are damp from the snow on the ground.

It's fucking obscene.

The voices and footsteps get closer, and I position myself in front of him. With our difference in size, I can't hide him, but I can block the more scandalous parts of him from view.

This is so far out of character that when I realize what I've done, it's jarring. Under normal circumstances, I would stand aside, wearing a smug grin and looking forward to seeing someone caught with their pants down.

But for reasons I'm not ready to unpack, I want to protect him. Want to save him from embarrassment and gouge out anyone's eyes that see him like this, breathless and desperate to fuck.

This side of him is only for me.

This is *mine.*

I try very hard not to read too deeply into that as an extremely wide-eyed Xalreth comes into view. As usual, Cadbury chases behind him with absolutely

G. Eilsel

no way to control the giant demon, and as he soaks in what he's seeing, rage lights his eyes.

CHAPTER 7

Niklaus

Xalreth's lip contorts into a snarl at the sight of Damien wearing my sweater, with me standing bare-chested behind him. "My Liege..." Unmistakable anger brews in his voice as he forces the words out of his clenched teeth. "Might I ask what the *fuck* is going on..."

Damien's spine snaps tall, and unbridled, suffocating power explodes out of him in a potent wave. It chokes me, my throat closing as my chest constricts with the weight pressing against every inch of my skin. Xalreth stumbles to a stop before slamming down onto a single knee before him, face low and neck exposed.

He *bows*.

For the first time, Damien doesn't look like a mere pampered prince, but the ruthless, cunning King of Hell he truly is. The monster behind the man is exposed.

A red, fiery aura pulses around Damien's frame as he takes a step closer. "Watch your fucking mouth." The sound is deeper and multi-dimensional, infused with the magic of his position, and Xalreth bows lower, forehead pressing against the snowy ground. "And mind your *fucking* business."

"Lucifer…" he gasps, fighting for his breath. "Forgive me, sir, it was…" Another choked, rasping inhale barely gives him any oxygen. "It was not my place."

"No," Damien says, still with that terrifying voice that seems to multiply, as though a thousand versions of himself are speaking at once, layering and mingling as he ripples with power. "It wasn't."

"Forgive me," Xalreth says again, and although the air remains thick with magic, Damien loosens his grip on his aura, allowing everyone to breathe.

For a long second, he stares at the back of Xalreth's bowed head, before heaving a sigh. "If you have something to say, say it now and be done with it."

Xalreth's black eyes finally lift, darting to me before focusing on Damien. The sheer amount of power he holds, despite his diminutive size, is enough to make my hair stand on end and my knees

Letters to Satan

ache to kneel before him as well. I'm barely able to resist the pull of submission.

All while his pants are soaked in his own cum.

Honestly, I'm impressed.

"Of course not, Lucifer, sir," Xalreth says, bowing his head subserviently once more. "It was a mistake to question your actions."

"Yes, it was." The oppressiveness surrounding us eases as Damien's temper is reined in, and he takes a step backward.

Xalreth's chest rises in a deep breath before he glances up at Damien again. "Does my king accept my most sincere apologies?"

Damien tsks, his usual saucy attitude returning as he crosses his arms and rolls his eyes. "Of fucking course I do. It has become a routine for you to behave like an idiot, and I always find it in myself to forgive you, don't I?"

"Yes, sir," Xalreth agrees, a small, relieved smile tugging at his lips as Damien gestures for him to rise and he climbs to his feet.

"Niklaus was about to introduce me to the reindeer," Damien says, snapping my attention back to him, "if you'd like to join us."

Was I?

Was I *really*?

Because this sounds *very* different from what I was imagining. My plan had been to haul his impudent ass to my bed and fuck him until he cried, then lick the tears off his flushed cheeks while I came inside him.

86

G. Eilsel

But if this is the game he's wanting to play, then I'll play.

"What a lovely idea, Lucifer," I say, and he smirks at the underlying threat in my voice. "Please, join us... Caddy, you're welcome to come along as well."

Understandably confused, Cadbury nods, probably wondering why I'm standing out here shirtless in the freezing snow. I'm nothing if not stubborn, though, and determined to hide my discomfort from Damien. "As you wish, Santa."

"Come, Lucifer," I purr, and his lip tugs up further at the double entendre.

"Aren't you cold?" he asks, falling in step beside me.

"Why, do you want to return my sweater? I'm sure Xalreth would have a few heated opinions about what he'd see if you did."

He laughs, pushing his hands up into the baggy sleeves and crossing them over his chest. "Nope, this is mine now."

Something possessive purrs inside my ribcage at the sight of him in my clothes, and I try to hide my smile, but fail miserably. We walk into the barn, and I don't miss the way his eyes light up at the reindeer in their stalls. In a jarring contrast to his earlier show of dominance, he now looks innocent and eager, almost youthful despite being centuries old.

He steps forward, then hesitates, and my grin downturns into a frown. "What's wrong?"

In a rare display of nerves, he licks his lips and gestures towards the reindeer, and I glance at the

Letters to Satan

enormous beasts. They are larger than most people realize, with fur that straddles the line between brown and gray. Soft, downy fuzz covers their noses, highlighted by the sun peeking through the windows.

"It's just that... animals aren't huge fans of demons. Most creatures avoid us and shy away, while others bolt and hide. On rare occasion, they even attack." He gave me a quick shrug, but his eyes reveal the unspoken hurt he tries to conceal.

My heart gives a sudden pinch in my chest.

How can such a powerful man be so *sweet*— turning into a sad boy because he can't cuddle all the animals? He yanks me from my thoughts when he adds, "Except cats, *obviously*. They adore demonkind."

Is that obvious?

Is it?

I open my mouth to question him when he gestures at the reindeer. "They probably won't like me." The disappointment in his tone causes my heart to give another funny squeeze, but I understand the sentiment better than most.

Being a leader means people respect you. They tolerate and obey, put on a smile when they're in your presence...

But it doesn't mean they like you.

And he encounters rejection not only from peers but also from animals, for no reason other than the way he was born. His very nature pushes them away, warns of the impending danger he carries.

It warns me, too.

So why do I want to get so close?

88

A burst of my magic is guided towards the reindeer, soothing them with its calming energy. "They're very friendly, and I'm sure they'll love you." I take his hand and tug him along, but resistance makes me stop, glancing over my shoulder at him.

Looking at our hands, he appears fascinated by the sight of our fingers weaving, like he's puzzled by how they fit together. His honey brown eyes move to mine, and for a fleeting moment, he's vulnerable.

But then, like it was nothing more than a trick of the light, his calm cockiness returns. "Everyone loves me."

"Of course they do," I tease, lips twitching as he walks up to my side, hand still woven with mine. He doesn't release me even as he reaches forward, tentative in a way he doesn't normally let others see. When his fingers land on the reindeer's snout, relief relaxes his posture before a sweet smile spreads over his lips. It nuzzles against his touch, and I can't bring myself to look away.

Fingers raking through my hair, I stare at the stacks of unfinished business and trashed deadlines that cover my desk. It feels like a lost cause, a desperate attempt to catch up on everything that's falling more and more behind.

How did I let myself get this far off schedule?

Letters to Satan

My preoccupation with Damien can't shoulder all the blame. Things were already running uncomfortably tight when he arrived on my doorstep, but now that he's here, my attention is even more scattered.

At this rate, we won't be done in time for Christmas, and that's never happened. It's not an option.

Exhausted, I scrub my hands down my face with a sigh, but a timid knock on my door interrupts my thoughts. "Santa?" Cadbury calls from the other side, and my fists clench in my hair before I take a calming breath, releasing the tension from my shoulders.

"Come on in." As soon as I spot his expression, I'm tempted to slam the door and pretend he was never here. "Gods..." I groan, slumping in my seat. "What is it?"

"Nothing major, sir... well, at least, I don't think it's major." Unable to find the energy to speak, I wave my hand, urging him to continue. "There seems to be a bit of a... record-keeping issue."

Yep, I should've slammed the door. "What *kind* of record-keeping issue?"

"Like I said, I don't believe it's anything major. When the elves working in the electronics department were pulling supplies, there were some tools and materials that were... well, *missing*, for lack of a better word. The problem is likely as minor as someone neglecting to sign the log, but I thought it was necessary to bring it to your attention."

G. Eilsel

A small frown tugs at my lips as I rub my forehead. "It's all electronics related?"

"Well, er... no..." he says, wringing his hands. "There are also a few missing heating elements and..." Cadbury pulls out a pocket-sized notebook and glances over the scribbles. "And quite a bit of silicone."

"Silicone?" My brows shoot up in surprise.

"Yes, sir... we use it for suction cups and figurines, amongst other things."

A headache threatens my temples as I shake my head, wishing I could fall asleep and wake to find this laundry list of problems solved. "Can you show me?"

"Of course, sir." Cadbury opens the door and gestures for me to go first, the quiet of the hallway contrasting with the symphony of sounds coming from the workshop.

Lost in thought, it takes my brain a moment to notice the elf with fire engine red hair walking past, causing me to do a double take and turn around to watch them. "Who was that?!"

"Oh, er... that was Mallow, sir, but she's going by Blayze with a Y now."

What the hell?

Jujube comes into sight, looking far more cheerful than usual, with a pep in his step that hasn't been there in years. "Yo, yo, Santa Daddy-O!" He's loud, words lilting with a strange accent I don't believe actually exists anywhere in the world. My brows dig deeper as I glance at the cut-out red H safety-pinned to his shirt.

Letters to Satan

What the actual fuck is going on around here?

Is this some sort of crazy fever dream?

Am I in a goddamned coma?!

Movement in the corner of my eye catches my attention, looking like it might come from the old Furby room. Right as I turn to look, Cadbury steers me into one of the storage rooms, and the thought slips away.

"This is where we've been finding the most discrepancies," he says, handing me the supply logs to review. Honestly, I'm not entirely sure what I'm searching for, but I fixate on the list of names as if it holds the answers and will share its secrets.

A few minutes pass, and I realize that staring at the logs isn't inspiring any dramatic breakthroughs, so I heave another tired sigh. "Will our production be impacted by the shortage?"

Cadbury shakes his head, taking the clipboard from my hands. "We'll be fine for Christmas this year."

That's one positive tally mark, at least.

"Alright. Remind the elves to handle logging their supplies with more care to avoid any more issues. And if anything else... strange... happens, let me know right away."

"Yes, sir, of course."

"Oh, is there a party in here I wasn't invited to?" Damien's cheerful voice rings out from behind me, and I turn to find him with a giant grin on his face, leaning against the doorframe with his arms crossed. He pushes off and takes a swaggering step towards me, absolutely coated in mischief.

"Why, Santa!" He puts his hand up beside his mouth as he whisper-shouts. "I didn't know you were still in the closet!" As soon as he says it, his eyes get wide with glee. "It's the Santa Claus-et!"

"Oh, my god," I mutter, dragging my hands over my face as I groan. "Never say that again." As I glance up at him, my grin grows wider at the sight of his proud smile beaming at me.

Then the fucker winks, and my brain goes fuzzy.

"Did you need something, Damien?" We haven't seen much of each other since our excursion to the reindeer barn yesterday. I've been up to my eyeballs in paperwork and deadlines, drowning in my impending doom.

Good times.

"Oh, well..." Hesitating, he appears almost shy, causing me equal parts surprise and skepticism. This timid version of him is incredibly suspicious... more suspicious than normal, even, and *that* is a feat.

His eyes finally land on mine as those blonde lashes flutter. "I was wondering if you wanted to have dinner. With me. Tonight."

My stomach flutters in response, but I clear my throat and attempt to keep my tone professional. "I suppose I owe you some time to discuss our ongoing issue."

His tongue flicks out between his lips as his eyes dart away... and is that a *blush* forming on his cheeks?

Holy shit, it is.

Letters to Satan

A maroon flush that almost hides his freckles paints his face, and I'm mesmerized by it.

"While that is true, I was hoping for something of more of a..." He pauses, those eyes like molten honey as he meets my gaze again. "Personal nature."

A satisfied smile plays on my lips as I step forward and grip his chin, tilting him towards me. "You wish to dine with me?"

"I do."

I lean closer, placing my mouth near his ear. "And does this dinner involve dessert?"

"Only the sweetest kind," he purrs back, and I press a barely-there kiss on the hinge of his jaw. A soft hum rises in his throat, not leaving his lips, and I move further until I pull the lobe of his ear between my teeth.

"Are you behaving?" I murmur as he shudders.

"Why does that feel like a trick question?"

I retreat and hold his gaze, so close we're nose-to-nose. "Why does that answer feel like side-stepping? What are you up to?"

He smiles, a sweet, serene thing that is just terribly full of suspicion. "I'm the Devil, Nik... I'm up to a lot of things. And if I play my cards right, sounds like I'll be..." His fingers tiptoe up my chest until they hook under the neck of my sweater and tug, pulling me forward until our lips brush. "Up to something *big* later."

"Trouble," I murmur, pressing a quick kiss to his lips before remembering that Cadbury is awkwardly standing to the side, pretending he isn't

G. Eilsel

witnessing this. "Be in my office at six-thirty sharp. Every minute you're late, you'll suffer the consequences."

"Oh, now, don't tempt me." A sly grin appears on his face as I raise a brow, and I push the sleeve of my sweater up a few inches, causing the muscles in my forearm to flex in warning. "Yes, sir, I'll be on time," he murmurs, tracing a finger along a vein on my arm before smiling to himself and walking away, tail twitching in a little wave goodbye.

Letters to Satan

CHAPTER 8

THREE STRIKES

Damien

Once I ensure Niklaus is safely out of the workshop, I linger for an extra five minutes before sneaking back into the Hellve's den. In a matter of days, the crew has gotten the entire production line operational, and boxes filled with finished products are neatly packed and ready for delivery.

Jujube stands at the front of the room, a miniature tyrant with his nose held high in the air like the aggravating little shit he is. "Lucifer, sir!" he shouts as I approach.

My eyes drift to the red H pinned on his shirt, a bold fashion choice that other Hellves have begun to imitate. A sudden surge of anger washes over me as I reach over and tear it off his chest, crumbling the paper in my fist.

Indignant, he protests, but I jab my finger between his eyes and watch as they cross. It would be comical if I wasn't so agitated. "You need to be more careful, and this?" I shake the crumbled paper badge in his face. "This is reckless. This is *idiotic.* The Santa is already suspicious that something is going on, and you want to flaunt your betrayal by parading around in that?"

"It'll be fine," he says, but I don't miss how he picks at the fuzz on his sweater, trying to hide the subtle tremble to his fingers. "Let me give you an update, sir." Even though it's an obvious distraction technique, it proves effective as he moves towards the production tables, and I fall in line behind him.

My stress about Niklaus discovering our operation diminishes when I glance at the table full of dongs, and I manage a smile.

"Our flagship item is the 'Candy Cane,'" he announces, displaying an eight-inch dildo with red and white stripes and a convenient curve at the tip. The silicone dick flops around, wobbling as he picks it up and waves it through the air. He grins wickedly as he slams it onto the table, the suction cup making a satisfying click as it latches to the metal.

"Second is the 'Knot Your Daddy's Christmas.'" This one is golden and swirled, shorter but thicker than the previous model, and a giant werewolf knot swells at the base.

Letters to Satan

He leads me through the lineup, from 'The Grinch' to the 'Cum Down Your Chimney,' complete with a reservoir for fake jizz that pumps from an almost invisible slit. The table ends with the 'Two-Turtled Dove,' a double ended dildo for when you feel like sharing the love.

I pick up a pair of clamps with tiny red bows on them we've been calling 'Jack Frost Nipping.' "I tested those," Jujube whispers, leaning close as he absentmindedly rubs at his nipples, wincing. "That hurts, bro. You sure people actually want that?"

"First, I'm not your bro," I say while baring my teeth at him, "and second, yes, they most certainly do."

"What about this?" He holds up a cock cage, twirling it around in his hand.

"The 'Chestnuts Roasting in an Open Wire?' Yes, just trust that I wouldn't have you making it if there wasn't a demand. This is my area of expertise, after all."

Our last stop is to a table full of butt plugs, bedazzled with red, green, and gold gems on the base. We're wavering between calling them 'Decked Halls' and 'Holey Pornaments.'

Choices, choices.

My eyes sweep the room at the roughly twenty elves, scurrying around as they work on crafting sex toys that are comically large in their tiny hands.

This should be funny, right?

Hilarious.

G. Eilsel

Instead of amusement, a sharp pang of guilt pierces through me, square in the chest. My hand moves to my sternum, rubbing the ridiculous feeling away before turning back to Jujube.

"Have Santa or Cadbury noticed the missing elves? Has anyone heard if they've started asking questions?"

Waving me off with a shrug, he shakes his head. "We're working in shifts and covering for each other in the workshop. Honestly, those goody-two-shoes are too busy trying to meet their quotas to pay any attention to us."

Another of those foreign pinches of guilt squeezes my insides as I shift uncomfortably. The consequences of losing a chunk of his workforce hadn't crossed my mind, and now I'm left feeling strange. Icky and slimy and, ugh...

Ashamed.

"Quotas?" I ask, trying my best to keep this churning in my gut to myself. "Are those still being met?"

"Dunno!" he says without a worry in the world, and my lips pull into a grimace. It doesn't matter that I'm holding up his production, right?

Right?

Why should I care?

Chest uncomfortably tight, I take one last glance at the boxes of finished products, my initial amusement at seeing them fading. "I have plans for the evening and need to be on my way. Stay on top of your other work, too, and tell the others to do the same. Falling behind on production could raise suspicions from Santa and risk the entire operation."

"Yeah, yeah, bro."

Temper flaring, I whirl to him and allow a tendril of my magic to escape, the slight static shock of it electrifying the air as it surrounds the terrified elf. "I told you I am not your bro."

Jujube's eyes get so wide, I'm concerned for a moment that they might pop out of his stupid little head. It would serve him right, treating me so familiar.

As though we are *equals.*

While I'm considering the pros and cons of popping his head like a pimple—with the biggest con being cleanup, obviously—the rest of the room falls deathly silent. I turn to find every eye warily staring at me, including Xalreth, who stands near the door as if he just entered.

Without a word, I storm out, barely taking the time to make sure no one is watching before I navigate through the workshop. In a manner completely unbefitting The Lucifer, I don't stop to cause trouble. There are no pranks or sabotage. I don't even bother with any snide remarks as I make my way to my room.

As I close the door behind me, I fall against it and take a deep breath.

What the fuck is the matter with me?

I can't help it.

Really, truly, I can't.

Since six twenty-eight, I've been lingering outside Niklaus's office, but the idea of being at the receiving end of his punishment is too thrilling to resist. Filthy thoughts swirl in my mind as I anticipate the consequences.

Will he tie me up?

Choke me until I'm on the verge of passing out?

Mark me?

Fuck, all the above?

My cock twitches in my pants at the prospect, and I stand here, almost dizzy with excitement, until the clock reads six thirty-three. Only three minutes late, but something tells me it'll be enough to have him flustered.

I rap my knuckles on the door in a rhythm, and a curt, "Come in," is spoken from the other side.

Gods, I'm fucking giddy.

Schooling my face to be neutral, I open the door and slide inside his office. "Good evening, Niklaus." I take a deep inhale and nearly moan at the heavenly aroma. "Sweet baby Jeebus, that smells incredible."

Niklaus stands, signature stoic expression on his face as he unbuttons the sleeve cuffs of his button-up shirt. My eyes track every single detail as he rolls them up twice, his movements calculated and precise as he tucks them tight. The fabric is taut against his thick arms as he gives it a tug.

101

Letters to Satan

Dear god, the way the muscles in his forearms roll and bunch is enough to make me beg.

He moves deliberately, each step agonizingly slow, until he stands in front of me, forcing me to crane my neck to meet his gaze. I don't even blink as he leans down and presses a kiss to my lips, then trails to my ear.

"Three."

A thrill travels up my spine, but I do my best to keep it contained, smiling at him with a flutter of my lashes. "Three what, Nik?"

He backs up, a predatorial smile in place as he nudges my nose with his, then stands tall. Somehow, he seems even larger as he towers over me. "Are you hungry?" Calm as can be, he offers me his crooked arm, and I take it out of pure instinct. He guides me to a cozy table by the enormous fireplace, and we are serenaded by the crackling and popping of the burning logs.

I stare at the table, then up at his perfectly serene demeanor, then at the table once more. My mouth moves in silence a couple of times, before I finally scoff and say, "Aren't you going to..."

"Aren't I going to *what*, little prince?" His green eyes are locked on mine when I glance up at him, the undercurrent of a challenge burning deep inside them. "Please, sit and let's eat. This day has been never-ending, and I've worked up quite the appetite." The suggestive inflection to his voice sends another of those silky shudders up my back.

The plates are loaded with juicy steaks, their sear marks crisscrossed in a way that make them almost too perfect, with a dollop of herb butter melting on top. Fluffy mashed potatoes with whipped peaks sit next to fresh green beans, and suddenly my stomach is roaring.

"Hungry?" he asks, amusement in his grin as he takes a seat across from me.

"Starving," I answer, sliding my fork into my mouth and sucking in my cheeks as I pull the bite of steak off.

He gives a tiny self-satisfied smile as he glances down at his food. "I know this is a social call, but we need to discuss a few matters."

Nerves bolt through my body as I freeze, another bite halfway to my mouth. "Oh, uh, what matters?"

His eyebrows bunch like they do when he's trying to figure me out. "The letters," he drawls, suspicion painting his face. "They're the reason you came after all... even if they're not the reason you're staying."

"Listen to you, being all cocky. Maybe I'm staying because I enjoy having miniature servants running around doing my bidding."

"Your bidding?" My eyes snap up to his green ones, and I curse myself for the choice of words. "Tell me, Lucifer, what orders have you given my elves to fulfill on your behalf?"

Fuck, fuck, fuckity-fuck.

I lie better than this... I'm the *Devil*, for fuck's sake.

Quick to regain my composure, I detect a glimmer of recognition in his eyes even as I slide a

Letters to Satan

smirk onto my lips. "Well, the elves are very handy to have at my disposal, you know. I haven't had to cook for myself or do my laundry since I arrived."

"You expect me to believe you don't have minions tending to your every need in Hell?"

I grin, cutting a bite off my steak. "Okay, you've got me there."

"You're up to something."

Lips closed tight, I smile around my food and swallow. "I'm always up to something, darling."

He stares, assessing, for another few seconds before surprising me by moving on from the conversation. "My proposition for the letter issue is simple. We'll provide a worker to the supernatural mail center to help sort the letters. It shouldn't take more than an hour a day, I'd imagine, and we can split the duties by alternating days."

Slowly, I nod. "That sounds straightforward enough."

"The post office will appreciate the extra hands, as well, so long as there's no trouble caused." He gives me a hard stare, but I only grin before he continues. "Any letters intended for me but mistakenly addressed to you will be intercepted and redirected."

"That's a reasonable solution," I agree, a heaviness settling in my gut.

"Of course, a few might sneak through. If that happens, perhaps you could... find *someone* to deliver them to me here, or I could send someone down to collect them."

104

G. Eilsel

"Oh? You want me to dispatch a liaison up here every time a dumb human misspells your name?"

"No," he says, gaze locked on mine. "I was hoping you'd come yourself."

I suck in a sharp inhale at the hunger in his eyes, and I slide my chair back with a loud scrape, preparing to pounce. He clicks his tongue, and I freeze, hovering just an inch above my seat. "Finish your meal, Damien."

"But..." A whine crawls from my throat, but he only chuckles as he returns his focus to his food.

"My god, how I love you needy," he says, reaching down to adjust himself under the table while I watch. My lips part in another desperate inhale, wanting to see more.

"Nik," I moan, my cock stiffening behind my pants, but he only smirks and nods towards my plate. He watches, satisfied, as I squirm in my seat until I've eaten every bite.

Dinner is deemed finished as he stands, and I almost lose it at the outline of his thick cock bulging against his pants. There's a predatorial glint in his eyes as he walks over and grabs the arms of my chair, spinning me with a loud drag of wood until I face him. My face is level with his erection, and I whimper at the size of him. "Are you ready for dessert?"

"Fuck yes, I'm so ready," I moan, reaching for him, but he snatches my wrist in midair.

"Did I give you permission to touch?"

Oh, my fuck yes.

Letters to Satan

Tingles shoot through my body at the rasp of his voice, and I tilt my face up to stare at him. "No, Daddy, you didn't." He doesn't stop me as I lean forward, pressing my cheek against his cock and rubbing up and down. His lip twists in a snarl as he wraps his hand around my head and tugs me closer, giving a slow, controlled thrust against me.

"What's your safe word?"

"I won't need it," I say, breathier than I mean to be.

"That wasn't the question, Damien. What is your safe word?"

"Pitchfork."

He smirks, but nods. "I want you naked." I look up and meet his eyes again, and he raises a brow at me, daring me to argue.

Without a word, I stand and tear my shirt over my head, then unbutton my pants and push them to the ground. Another snarl rips onto his lip, this one joined by a growl, at the black lacy thong I'm wearing.

"Do you want me to take this off, too?" I ask, sliding my thumbs through the lace bands and tugging as I shimmy my hips.

His tongue flicks between his lips, nostrils flaring as he stares at my hard cock trapped under the fabric.

"Leave it," he growls, turning and walking away. I blink a few times at his retreating frame, confused. Leather creaks as he drops into the seat behind his desk, his eyes finding me again as he

G. Eilsel

adjusts himself, giving a subtle stroke through his pants.

"Come, little prince." My hand lands on my cock and I drag it along my length, tipping my head up with a soft moan. Niklaus leans forward with a warning rumble low in his throat. "I will not ask a second time."

I strut over, my knees falling onto either side of his hips as I climb into his lap. He palms my ass cheeks, fingers slipping underneath the tiny strip of fabric and coasting up and down before snapping it against my skin.

His hand comes around to my face, two fingers hovering in front of my lips, and I open obediently. He pushes them into my mouth, and I try to suck, but he shoves them deeper until they're bumping the back of my throat and making me gag.

"Oh, this pretty mouth is going to have to do better than that," he muses as he keeps thrusting. Spit dribbles out the sides of my lips as I tilt my chin, sucking his fingers hard enough to hollow my cheeks. His cock stabs against me as he finger-fucks my mouth, never looking away.

I suck in a deep, gasping breath when he yanks his hand back. Spit drips off his fingers and he wipes them gently over the skin of my cheek. It's filthy and strangely tender at the same time, and it makes my heart thud in my chest. His eyes pinch as he swipes through the mess on my face. "Look at you," he murmurs, gaze soft and voice rough.

I only whimper, but it seems to be enough for him.

Letters to Satan

"Stand," he commands, and I scramble to my feet as he rises from his chair. Harsh hands spin me and his grip on my neck shoves my torso until I'm bent over in front of him. Fully clothed, he rolls his hips against me, my cheek pressed into the desk. "Wrap your tail around your wrist. If it interrupts me, we start all over again."

My body jolts with a sharp sting as his palm meets my ass in a slap, the smack of skin ringing through the room. "Count for me, little prince."

"Wha-what?" I ask, trying to look at him, but he holds me steady. After a pause, he lets out a sigh that indicates his dwindling patience with me is faltering.

A palm slides up my cheek, rubbing where he just struck me. "We'll have to start over then, won't we?" He spanks me again, the sting like lightning up my spine.

"One!" I gasp, and his chuckle is dark.

"See? You are a quick learner."

Another slap to my ass cheek has me whimpering and my cock rages, pushing against the silky material of my panties. "Two," I grit out, the heat of his hand a brand on my skin.

"And how many do you get?"

"Three," I whisper.

"That's right," he soothes, rubbing the tender skin with his palm before giving a final spanking that has me arching my back and shouting. He kicks my foot and my legs spread wider as he releases my neck. "Stay right there and do not move." He drops to his knees behind me, licking and kissing along the

108

blistered flesh of my ass before moving towards the center.

"Look at this tight little hole, just waiting to be stretched and stuffed full of me."

"Please... *please*," I beg, wiggling as he chuckles and slips a finger underneath the fabric of my thong again. Tugging it aside, the velvety heat of his tongue glides across my hole, and it flutters as I search for more. A loud, desperate noise claws its way from my throat as he licks, sweeping in patient, steady strokes.

The scrub of his beard between my ass cheeks scrapes the skin angry and raw, but I've never loved the friction as much as I do right now. One of his hands lands on each of my cheeks and he spreads me, rolling his tongue as my asshole clenches, searching to be filled.

"Please, Daddy, more... give me more," I beg, and his laugh vibrates over my skin.

When the tip of his tongue spears inside me, I buck backward, shamelessly grinding against him as he works me open. Fingers dig into the muscles of my ass as he spreads me further, working himself deeper with determined thrusts. He releases one hand and reaches around, sliding his fingers inside my underwear to grip my cock.

I spasm as if I've been electrocuted, an inhuman howl leaving my throat.

Nonsense spills from my lips. Begging and pleading, shouting his name and asking for more as he eats me out, never stopping his steady strokes. Unparalleled ecstasy ripples through me, pleasure

Letters to Satan

like I've never felt catapulting me into desperate oblivion. Nothing in the world matters anymore—nothing beyond the warm drag of his tongue and the stroke of his hand.

My hips roll, fucking myself against his face as my balls draw tight and my cock swells in his fist. Tense, delicious heat builds in the base of my spine, and I'm shameless as I chase that high. "Nik... fuck, Nik, I'm about to, I'm going to..." All at once, mere milliseconds before I explode, he tears his mouth away and stills his hand. A firm grip squeezes at the base of my cock, denying me at the last moment.

Confused, my body continues to pulse even as the orgasm is cut off, and I wail, trying to fuck into his grip. Another dark, satisfied chuckle reaches my ear as he pins me in place. A steady stream of pre-cum leaks down my shaft and over his fingers, and he squeezes my cock when he feels it.

"Someone's a leaky boy, aren't they?" He pulls his hand away, my climax denied, and I whine as I reach for myself. With a click of his tongue, he grabs my wrist and spins me to face him, still on his knees. He stands, towering over me, then leans in to my ear.

"One."

CHAPTER 9

ROUGH AROUND THE EDGES

Niklaus

The shock on Damien's face is enough to make me smile as I pull back. He's fucking glorious, cheeks flushed a deep maroon, chest heaving, ass slick with spit, and his cock pushing against his lacy little panties. It's so hard that I don't know how it's even still contained, with every contour on full display.

"One?" Realization dawns on his face, quickly morphing into an emotion somewhere between fury and desperation.

I nod, dropping back into my chair and gripping my cock through my pants. The tiny touch of

Letters to Satan

friction sends sparks through my limbs, and I'm so hard it hurts, but I have to be patient.

Such a shame that his punishment is just beginning.

"Come here, Damien." He snarls and crosses his arms over his chest, refusing, and I slide my eyes over his delicious, lithe body. "If you don't listen, we'll be forced to start over."

Arms still crossed and tail twitching in agitation, he makes a show of his displeasure as he stomps over to stand in front of me. My fingers dig into his hips as I spin him, running my palm over the handprint burning red on his ass and giving it another tap. I tug him into my lap, eyes rolling back in my head at the sensation of my cock rubbing against him.

A soft moan climbs from his lips as I roll up into him, and I bind my arm around his torso, pulling him back until he's laying against my chest.

"Put your feet on my knees." I reach in a drawer for a bottle of lube, and this time, he listens, drawing his legs up and letting his body slouch, tail drooping to the ground.

I yank his knees apart, spreading him wide open. "That door isn't locked," I mutter in his ear as I lick up the slope of his neck. "Anyone could come in here and watch you getting fucked. How does that make you feel?"

He whimpers and spreads his legs even further, and I chuckle as his cock flexes against his panties. "Good boy," I purr as I flick the lid of the lube open and move it to his hole.

G. Eilsel

"Oh, shit," he gasps as I push the tip inside him and squeeze, letting the slick liquid fill his ass. I toss the bottle aside as I bite at his ear.

"Do you feel it dripping out of you?"

"Fuck, yes," he moans, his hips trying to arch into the air.

"Get used to that, Damien... that slow drip out of your pretty little hole. It's going to be your permanent state of existence around me." My hand skates down the front of his body until I reach his soaked hole, slipping one finger inside him easily.

There's an obscene, wet *schlick* as I thrust into him, and he moans as I work a second finger past his rim. "This is when you came in your pants last time, little prince. You're going to have to take more of me tonight, though."

His blonde curls muss against my pecs as he nods, and I slide in and out of his hole. He clenches, gripping me as I finger-fuck him. Loud, wailing moans leave his throat as I curl my fingers and sink inside his heat, finding his prostate as he writhes in my lap. My arm binds him tighter as he squirms, attempting to fuck himself on my hand.

"You are such a needy little thing, aren't you?" I murmur in his ear as I press a third finger against his hole. "So fucking hungry for my cock."

Lube slicks his skin and mine as I stretch him, obsessed with the way his body yields for me. Once all three fingers slip past his rim, I pull out before thrusting back in. He wails as his cock strains against his soaked panties, the fabric shiny with his pre-cum.

113

Letters to Satan

Knuckle deep, I hold there for a few seconds while he whimpers and tries to move, begging with both his words and his body. The muscles in his thighs shake, his limbs shivering with the fullness. I withdraw until my fingers are barely inside him before driving forward again, and he cries my name so loudly, I know it's bouncing down the hallways.

Anyone outside could hear him at my mercy.

I want them to hear.

Want them to know he's mine.

Again and again, I thrust into him, and he clenches around me as his cock tenses, hard as granite under his lace. A strained shout is forced from between his teeth, then I pull out of him and pin him in place as he sobs. His hips jerk as he tries to send himself over the edge, arms pinned against him as he thrashes.

I chuckle in his ear, enjoying the way he squirms. "Two."

"Nik, please let me," he whines, still trying to thrust as more of his thick pre-cum beads through his underwear, rolling down his length. "*Please*, I learned my lesson."

"Oh, I very much doubt that," I murmur. "You knew the consequences of being late."

"Please." He whips his head around to stare at me with wide, wild eyes, and I dig my fingers into his blonde curls and crush his lips to mine. This kiss is hungry, *starving*, full of lips and teeth and tongues, and when I trust he won't come from a single touch, I loosen my hold on his body.

114

G. Eilsel

"Get on the desk and show me that loose, needy hole." His eyes are hooded as his head lulls and his gaze meets mine, looking almost drunk with his need. When he doesn't move fast enough for me, I stand and pick him up, placing him on top of the desk with another kiss. "Lay back and spread yourself out for me."

He falls onto his back, papers and pens scattering as I grab his thighs and yank him to the edge of the desktop. I push his knees, exposing his opened hole to me.

"Such a fucking beautiful little slut." I slide my thumb around his thong, slipping inside him as he moans. "So wet and ready for Daddy's cock."

"Yes, please, I need it," he whines, and I grin at his submission as I reach down and unzip my pants, working my aching cock through the fly. The lube creaks as I open it a second time, pressing the tip of the bottle into his hole and squeezing again.

Clear liquid slides out of him as he breathes in stuttered exhales, and then with no warning, I line us up and shove myself all the way inside.

Body jolting from the impact, he's keening—wailing and crying and cursing—as I wrap my hands around his hips and slam into him again. He's warm and tight, mouth sagged open and eyes fluttering closed as his tail twitches like it doesn't know what to do. "You're so fucking big," he breathes out as I lean forward, hooking his knees with my elbows and folding him in half as I fuck him harder.

I inch closer until we're nose to nose. "Who do you belong to?"

Letters to Satan

"You... you, I'm yours... yours." I growl and slide my arms underneath his body, lifting him off the desk while I'm still speared deep inside him.

"Who *owns* you, little prince?"

"You do," he wails as I move him up and down my cock.

"That's right, I do. And if I want to use you like a cock sleeve and fuck you until you're stretched and full, I'll do it. This hole? It's mine." His head falls back like he's too weak to keep it up, trusting me to hold him as I use him. Our skin slaps together in loud claps, sweat beading on my forehead and trickling down my temples.

Every slide of his warm body has me toeing closer to the line, and half of me is tempted to give in to what both of us want. But the other half—the more disciplined one—knows that he hasn't paid for the minutes he kept me waiting.

His intention was obvious when he did it. He wanted to provoke me... wanted the punishment. It's not like I couldn't hear him in the hallway, killing time just to be a brat. I turn and press him against the wall, his head thunking back as I fuck him harder, wedging his cock between us.

"Fuck, Nik, fuck you feel so good," he moans, and he's so tight I can feel it as he clenches around me, ready to blow. Forcing my brain to override my body, I wait until the last second and deny him one final time. I pull out, leaving him suspended in my arms, his needy hole pulsing around nothing.

"No!" Voice cracking, his tail lashes out, lassoing my waist and trying to tug me closer.

"Have we learned our lesson yet?"

"Yes," he sobs.

"Yes, *what?*"

"Yes, Daddy!" I snarl and growl as I lean in to capture his lips, carrying him back to the desk. His feet hit the floor as I flip him around and bend him over, white-knuckling the edge of the desktop to brace himself as I thrust into him.

Back arching, he meets my every thrust as the slick sounds of our bodies meeting fills the entire room. I need him in a way I've never experienced... need to be so deep that we can never be separated. It's all-consuming, and I grab his hips and lift them off the ground, trying to get deeper.

He scrambles for balance as his chest falls against the desk, and I bury myself, giving in to the pull of his body while his feet hang before me. I want to be under his skin and in his very blood... for there to be no way to tell where I end and he begins.

"Who's my good little cock sleeve?" I fuck him hard enough to make him call out, watching the bounce of his pert ass as it ripples.

Muscles in his back flex as he squirms in my grip, his voice a series of gasps. "I am... I'm your good little hole. Please, Nik, *please*. I'm nothing but a hole for you."

"That's right, you're *my* hole. Does my hole want me to use it?"

"Use me, Daddy, please," he moans as he flexes around me. "Fill me... mark me." Even worked open and loose, he's so tight that his every reaction is amplified, squeezing and contracting along my cock

Letters to Satan

as I drive into him. Timid, he dances on this line once again, unsure if I'll allow him to finish or not.

Just the way I like him.

"Nik... oh, fuck, Nik..." He chants my name as the contractions around my cock get faster, more powerful, and then his thighs tremble as he sucks in a deep breath and holds it, body shaking. His hole tightens as the air is punched from his lungs, and he comes with so much force that it sprays through the fabric of his panties, painting the top of my desk.

The sounds he makes are feral, completely obscene, and so satisfying I could sustain myself indefinitely off them.

"That's my good little prince." I stop holding back, my fingers digging pits into his hips. My body is so tight, my insides are twisted into knots, my toes and fingers curled into talons as the pressure builds to breaking. All at once, relief crashes through me in a wave, and I roar as I slam forward, bottoming out inside him as my cock jerks with my release.

I hold him there, listening to his keening mewls, as pleasure like I've never known almost brings me to my knees.

After the initial blinding waves roll through my body, I give a few steady pumps as I savor the rest of my orgasm. Damien is a whimpering mess spread out on the desk, still speared on my cock and at my mercy. My chest rises in a few deep breaths as I calm my racing heart, letting reality set in once again.

Once I place his feet on the ground, I pull out and kneel behind him, enamored as I watch streams of cum leak out of his abused hole.

My hole.

I scoop some of my cum onto two fingers and gently push it inside him, and his soft moans are laced in exhaustion.

"I came all over the naughty list," he rasps, and I huff a deep laugh at the way his body is melted over the surface. He's boneless and unwilling to move as he flops there, breath labored and skin clammy with sweat. I press a line of kisses up his spine and then scoop him up, taking him through a door no one but me is permitted to enter.

Letters to Satan

CHAPTER 10

PAMPERED PRINCE OF HELL

Damien

I'm dead.

Deceased.

He's killed me.

There's no other explanation, because my body is made of lead, and I can't find the energy to move even a finger. Niklaus scoops me up, my nerves buzzing and ass burning as his cum slides out of me, and god only knows where it's landing. I'm like fucking Hansel or Gretal, leaving a breadcrumb trail of his jizz that keeps leaking from my ass.

Too exhausted to hold on, I nuzzle into the coarse hair on his chest and close my eyes as he carries me. A door clicks and I peek out of one eye, finding us in a cozy bedroom with a giant bed and roaring fire.

"What are we doing?" I murmur, my lips barely moving.

He balances me with one hand, but my eyes drift shut again, only half conscious as I'm lowered onto a pillowy mattress and surrounded by his scent. Cinnamon and clove with a hint of smokiness, and I breathe deep as my heavy limbs sink into the comfort.

"Did I hurt you?" Niklaus asks, voice surprisingly tender as the bed dips beside me, and I crack a single eye open. His shirt is off, but his pants are still on, unbuttoned and unzipped, and although he's tucked himself away, obvious streaks of cum stripe the fabric around the fly. My dick gives a feeble attempt at rising before telling me to fuck off and promptly going back to sleep.

"You hurt my balls when you kept edging me," I mumble, and he chuckles as he grips my chin and tilts my face to his. These funny pangs in my chest are getting worse, more intense, the more time I spend with him, and I'm not sure how to feel about it.

He says nothing, just watches me for a moment before leaning in to kiss me. "You're going to destroy me," he whispers, something forbidden in his eyes, and rises from the bed.

"Nik?" I whisper, but he acts like he doesn't hear me and walks through a door. Debating whether to follow him, and questioning why I want to, I pull my lip between my teeth. Relationships are a luxury I

Letters to Satan

cannot afford to have. The responsibilities of ruling the realm allow little time for even a quick fuck to ease the tension.

I know where my duties lie.

So why have I been hiding out here for the past week, playing house with him?

Before I can convince myself to get up and leave, show him exactly where we stand, he enters the bedroom wearing a pair of flannel pants slung low on his hips, carrying a glass of water and a cloth. Wordlessly, he hands me the cup and peels my sticky underwear down my legs, wiping me clean before lifting my knees and inspecting my ass.

It's terrifyingly intimate.

"I'm fine," I insist, but he ignores me and gently cleans me before leaning in to place a soft kiss on my thigh. When he scoops me up again, my eyebrows knit. "Where are you taking me now?" Out, I'd wager. Anywhere but here, in his space. Now that the sex is done, I suppose he has no more use for me.

It's understandable, but fuck... why does it sting so much?

He pushes through another door and warm, humid air coats my skin as the sound of running water fills the room. A hint of a smile softens his rugged face as he carries me over to an enormous bathtub. "A prince has to be pampered. It's part of the rules, or so I hear."

For a second, I stare at the water, with tiny salt crystals visible in the bottom of the tub. A small bath pillow rests on one side and a candle flickers on the other, and to my absolute *horror*, the sting of tears burns behind my eyes.

"Where's my wine and grapes?" I ask, a sniffle breaking free beyond my control.

A sniffle.

I am The Devil... The Lord of the motherfucking Underworld, and I'm snivelling like a baby because he ran me a bath?

He hums, an amused sound, before he finally puts me on my feet. At least he's allowing me the dignity of stepping into my bath instead of dropping me in like an overgrown sperm. "Do you want a glass of wine, Damien? I didn't think you'd be hungry after that dinner, but we worked up quite the appetite."

A grin digs into my cheeks as I glance up at him, his green eyes softer than usual. When he reaches over to shut the water off, I expect him to leave, but he grabs a washcloth and dips it into the tub, nudging me to lean forward as he drags the steaming water over my back.

"You don't have to wash me... I'm not a child," I protest, even though every muscle in my body relaxes into his touch.

There is a sarcastic edge to his chuckle. "Oh, you most certainly are not, my little prince. You've ruled over Hell for nearly two hundred years. I'd daresay you've warmed that throne longer than multiple generations of my family have been on this Earth."

"Were you not related to the previous Santa?" While I lack precise details, I know the former Santa Claus served for almost eighty years, a short period

Letters to Satan

for a supernatural leader. The transition of power was done quietly, and until now, there wasn't much information about the man who took his place.

The man currently washing my hair.

"I wasn't," he says, wringing out the washcloth and letting the water shower over my head. "Traditionally, these positions are passed among families, but there have been instances where that wasn't true. In those cases, and mine, it was because there was no living heir to inherit the position. Most people don't realize that a handful of humans have lived in the North Pole over the years. My mother was one of those humans."

"Is she still here?"

"No," he says, a hint of sadness in his voice. "The previous Santa, Bernard... he and my mother were in love, but she refused to marry him. To do so would've allowed her to assume his magic, and with it, his lifespan. But she had me, and I was only human. She wouldn't take on his long life without a means to do it for her son, and no way is known to pass the magic to anyone besides a spouse or biological child."

"He wasn't your father?"

"No, my father died when I was very young. My mother was struggling with being a single parent, and she stumbled upon Bernard leaving presents in our home when I was only a few years old. He claims he never heard her coming, but I have my doubts."

"You think he planned it?" I ask as he finishes washing me and sits back on his feet.

124

G. Eilsel

"Yes, I do," he says, a nostalgic smile crossing his lips. "I believe he saw her the previous Christmas and decided he wanted her for himself, then made enough noise that she'd wake and find him in the living room. He always was a hopeless romantic."

"So he brought you both to the North Pole to live?"

"Yes. I was a giant among elves."

"And they never had children of their own."

"No," he says, scooping water over my arms to rinse the suds from my skin. "He was a good man... fair. Didn't want me to feel as though I had to compete for his love. And Mom would not have agreed to have more children, anyway. She was older when I was born and always complained I had too big of a head to go through that again."

I grin as I lean back, sinking into the steaming water. "What happened to your mother?"

"She died, eventually. Peacefully, in her old age, surrounded by those she loved. And once she did, Bernard didn't want to live this long life without her. He passed the magic to me and chose to follow her out of this life."

"The magic works that fast? If you decided to no longer be The Santa, you'd die?"

"No, sweet Damien, I wouldn't die." My heart sputters again at his words.

Sweet?

Me?

Throughout my life, I've been called many awful, spiteful things that are... possibly mostly true. I *am* the devil, after all. The actions I take on a

125

Letters to Satan

random Tuesday would probably haunt most people for years. I'm evil. Conniving.

But sweet?

I could be sweet for him. I immediately freeze as the thought registers in my brain.

He doesn't notice my conflict as he continues with his story. "The magic doesn't stop your aging, just significantly slows it. The longest living Santa in our history stepped down after almost six hundred years in the position. Bernard had been in the office many decades and could've kept living for another several centuries or more. When he passed the title along, he told me the magic gave him a choice. Pick up where he'd been in age, which in his case would've been his mid-sixties, or let the years catch up to him." He waves his hand through the air vaguely. "He chose to move on."

"How long will you hold the title?"

"You mean, how long will I live?"

"They go hand in hand."

He stares at me for a long second. "As long as I have something to live for, Damien."

I hesitate as I lean forward, resting my arms over the side of the tub. "And do you have something to live for right now, Nik?"

"I've been asking myself that a lot recently."

"Don't you love the position? Being The Santa?"

"I do... growing up here, in this setting and around these people, has given me a unique view of life, that's for sure. But at the end of the day, it's not about me. It's about everyone else and bringing joy to those that need it... like how Bernard brought joy to my mother."

"What, so you're going to kidnap yourself a bride?"

He snorts and grins, and I can't help it as my lips pull up in a smile as well. "Smartass," he mutters, shaking his head.

"You bring me joy," I say without thinking, then flinch as he tilts his head, staring. And holy fuck, I want to rewind time by a few seconds and take that back, because not only is it something the Devil should never be caught saying, but it's goddamned *embarrassing*. "I just... I just mean that... this thing between us... this is fun, you know?"

"Fun? That's all this is?"

"It's all it can be."

He gives a noncommittal hum, like he isn't convinced. "Tell me, Damien... do you enjoy your position?"

"Yes." It's a given, an automatic response, and I stop and make myself really consider what he's asking. The identity of The Lucifer has been a part of me for so long that it's woven into the fabric of my being. I don't know what it's like to not be in charge of the realm after two centuries.

What would it be like, not dealing with the headaches that come with being pulled in so many different directions all the time? To not be weighed down by the stress of so much responsibility every moment of every day?

Letters to Satan

But it's not that simple. You can't just step away without considering the consequences—and there would be plenty.

It hits me all at once that I've gone days with not a single thought about the Underworld. I've barely even spoken to Xalreth and haven't asked for any updates from the realm.

"You don't sound convinced," Niklaus says, like my thoughts are broadcasting themselves.

"Of course I am," I snap, more out of frustration with myself than anything. "What, do you think I'd drop two centuries of duty and responsibilities to play house with you because you're a good lay? We are having fun, Nik, but that's all this is. Don't ruin it by wanting what you can't have."

Hurt flashes across his face before he masks it with a somber expression. He tears his eyes away and nods, busying himself by digging a towel from the cabinet. Guilt eats at my stomach, churning in my gut as I watch his jaw tense. "Take as long as you need," he says, and turns to walk out.

"Nik," I call after him, but he doesn't turn around, just closes the door behind him with a soft click. Foreign emotions swirl through my mind as I sit in the steaming bath, staring mindlessly at the stone tile on the wall. A mess of confused thoughts are trapped in my head, not knowing the answers to the questions he threw at me.

Am I happy?

Could I be happy?

Is that a luxury I deserve?

G. Eilsel

Water sluices down my body as I climb out of the tub and dry myself, wrapping the towel around my waist as I step into the bedroom. Nik sits on the edge of the bed, his back facing me as he flips through his phone, no doubt still working.

"Goodnight, then," he calls over his shoulder, and the pinch in my chest at the dismissal is more painful than it should be.

Steeling my spine, I walk over and tug the phone from his hands, and his face tilts to mine as I sit it on the table and wrap my arms around his neck, climbing on to straddle his lap. "I don't know how to be anything but the Devil," I whisper like a secret between us, leaning forward to kiss his lips as he relents and wraps his arms around me. "Don't know how to be sweet, or care for others, or not be a complete ass. I don't know how to do *this*."

"You don't give yourself enough credit, because you *are* sweet, and you care greatly for others. You just hide it by being an ass."

I raise a brow at him. "You aren't denying that part?" He shrugs, which makes both of us laugh, some of the tension dissipating. "Can I stay with you tonight?"

"You can stay with me as long as you'd like," he says, and fuck if my heart doesn't take a nosedive at those words. "I just have one request."

"What's that?"

"If you're going to break my heart, at least give me time to prepare. Can you do me that one courtesy?" Emerald eyes bore into mine, and all I can do is offer him a small nod as he pulls me in for

Letters to Satan

another kiss. I lose myself to the softness of his lips, and as his steady hands spin me to the bed beside him, I stop thinking and just allow myself to feel.

G. Eilsel

CHAPTER 11

UNDER THE TABLE

Niklaus

Christmas deadlines are pointed at me like the barrel of a gun, and I'm just waiting for someone to pull the trigger. Everything is behind schedule, and if things continue at the current rate they're going, we'll be at a three percent shortage come Christmas Eve.

It sounds so small, doesn't it? So insignificant.

But when you consider the sheer number of people on the planet, three percent starts to look a whole lot more substantial. Elf populations have dwindled in the past few decades, for no other reason than fewer children have been born. And

Letters to Satan

knowing this, knowing we would fall short, I failed to act.

My approach has been too lax, too *lenient*, all because I didn't want to upset the elves by asking them to put in the extra hours needed. I'm suffering the consequences of my own soft heart.

Cadbury's familiar knock taps against my door, and I invite him inside. "You wanted to see me, sir?"

"Yeah," I grunt, still staring at the endless papers before me.

"Sir?" he nudges, and I realize I've just been sitting in silence for a long stretch. "Is everything alright?"

"We're behind schedule, Caddy, and it's my fault."

"You can't shoulder all of that blame, sir. There are thousands of us here." He puts a hand on his hip as he raises a strict brow at me, anticipating my argument before it even forms on my lips.

"The elves will have to pick up extra shifts over the next week and a half, and even then, I'm not sure we're going to make it."

"You've never failed us, Niklaus, and I have every confidence this year will be no different. I'll speak with the department leaders about increasing hours. They'll do whatever it takes to help you. We are here to serve, sir. Don't forget that."

My chest rises with a deep breath as I attempt to latch onto the assurance in his words, but it's a struggle. I wasn't born into this life. Even though my mother and I came to live at the North Pole when I

G. Eilsel

was young, stepping into the role of Santa didn't come naturally to me. Bernard's abrupt passing has forced me to find my own way through the transition.

It has taken me years to become confident in the job, and I expect it will require many more years for me to be content with my progress. My discipline has always been my driving force, but now my emotions for Damien have clouded even that.

And speaking of the Devil...

"There will be a delegate from the supernatural mail system here later for a meeting with me and The Lucifer."

"Very well. I'll be on the lookout for their arrival." He hesitates, and when I glance at him, there's a familiar curiosity in his eyes. "How much longer do The Lucifer and his companion plan to stay in the North Pole?"

"Why? Is it causing issues?"

"No, no, it's just that... the elves have been talking and..." My hackles rise knowing they've been gossiping.

"And?" I ask, my voice colder than I intend.

"And, well, I can't help but wonder if he's a bad influence on the elves."

I sit back in my seat, pulling the side of my cheek between my teeth. "Has there been trouble I'm unaware of?"

"No, sir, but—"

"Has The Lucifer been causing problems, or disrupting work, or speaking inappropriately to the elves?"

"Not that I'm aware of—"

133

Letters to Satan

"Then what *exactly* is the problem?"

Caddy stares at me for a long second before he gives a slow shake of his head. "There is no problem."

"We don't have the luxury of idle gossip and running mouths while we're this far behind schedule. If there's time to indulge in rumors, they can find the time to help me get this Christmas caught up."

"Of course, sir," he says, bowing his head. "Is there anything else you need from me?"

"No, that's all." He bows again and leaves me to my thoughts, but they just keep returning to one place.

"Thank you for joining us today, Arryn," I say as I lead the shapeshifter into our formal dining area. The governing body for supernaturals is diverse, with representatives from all factions, but the communication department is primarily run by shapeshifters. This gives them the ability to move between realms unnoticed and blend into their surroundings.

Right now, Arryn appears as a human woman with long brown hair and a soft smile, and it's no doubt meant to put us at ease. Their natural appearance is much more sinister, with an unnaturally large mouth filled with needle-like teeth.

Not something you want to be on the wrong end of.

"I must say, everyone at the office was *very* intrigued when we received a request for a joint meeting with The Santa and The Lucifer. It was quite the competition to decide who would attend." Her eyes take a slow perusal up my body, an obvious suggestion in them.

Damien narrows his eyes at her. "And how did you win?"

She flashes him another of those unnervingly serene smiles. "Brute force, naturally."

"Naturally." He matches her sinister smile with one of his own, and I clear my throat before either of them gets any wild ideas about testing their strength. I don't think Arryn would be stupid enough to challenge Damien, but one never knows.

People are always a little dumber than we give them credit for.

My hand lands on the small of Damien's back, and I steer him towards the table and pull his chair out for him. Arryn's brows fly up, but she smartly doesn't say a word. She sits before I can offer the same courtesy to her, and I take my seat right as a group of elves walks in with our meal.

Once everything is sat in front of us, I gesture at the food—a shrimp scampi with asparagus that smells divine. "Please, this is informal. Eat while we talk." She nods and takes a bite, letting her eyes roll up in her head as she releases a delighted moan.

"It's amazing, isn't it?" Damien purrs as he leans over and grips my forearm, giving it a light

Letters to Satan

squeeze. "Nik—oh, excuse me, The Santa is so good at spoiling his guests."

"And... how long have you been a guest here?" she asks, cocking her brow as she takes another bite.

"Long enough to be *quite* spoiled." He slides his fork between his lips and holy fuck, it should not be as provocative as it is.

I put some warning into my throat clearing, and he glances over and tosses me a wink. "We've called you here to discuss some distribution issues with the mail system... although it's no fault of yours," I quickly add as I see her defenses rise. "It's mere human error, but something we really can't eliminate at the source."

Placated, she settles back into her chair and gestures for me to continue. "Alright, I'm listening." Startled by a light touch on my leg, I glance down to find Damien's tail flicking playfully on the inside of my calf.

"Something wrong, Nik?" he asks as it skates higher, swirling in circles around my knee.

A second clearing of my throat gives me the composure to smile calmly. "Of course not, I apologize. The Lucifer has been getting the occasional letter mistakenly made out to *Satan* instead of *Santa*, and it is becoming a hindrance."

"Just how many letters are you receiving for it to be a problem, Lucifer?"

I open my mouth, but he speaks over me as his tail lashes against my thigh like a whip, and I suck in a sharp breath at the sting. "Enough for it to be annoying, and enough for me to deem it needs to be fixed."

"Alright, I'll bite. What exactly do you want us to do about it?"

"We've thought that through as well," I say, attempting to maintain my poker face as Damien's tail slithers up my thigh like a snake, my cheeks heating as it brushes between my legs. "Da—The Lucifer and I have agreed to split a task force. One of his minions or one of my elves will help sort through his intended mail for the day and reroute any letters that are obviously meant for me."

"Obvious how?" she asks, and I shudder as his tail drags up the length of my cock.

"Oh, you know," he purrs, stroking in a rhythm now. "Anything with candy stripes or Christmas trees drawn on the envelope." My knees spread as I scoot forward in my seat, giving him access as my erection pushes against my pants. His smile is scandalous as he leans his elbows on the table.

"Alright, that makes sense, but some will still sneak through."

"You just let me take care of those." Damien tosses her a wink as she shrugs.

"I see no issue with it, provided that they finish sorting before the mail is sent out and don't impede the workers."

"Fantastic!" Damien says with a giant smile. Up and down, his tail strokes me, and I'm content for him to carry the conversation as I soak in the pleasure that's rippling through my body.

Letters to Satan

"Well, this was... surprisingly uneventful," Arryn says, unaware of what's happening under the table. Something tells me if she knew, her opinion about the eventfulness of this dinner would change in a heartbeat. "While I'm here, do you think I could see the workshop? Check it off my bucket list?"

"Uh, of course," I stutter, trying to figure out how to stand without putting my rock-hard cock on display, when Damien solves my conundrum and yells for Cadbury.

Mere seconds later, his head pops in the door. "You rang, Lucifer?"

Damien's catty grin suggests he is enjoying having my staff at his beck and call. I shake my head and turn to Cadbury. "Would you be so kind as to offer Ms. Arryn here a tour of the workshop?"

"Of course, sir." He gives her a cheerful smile, which she returns as she stands from her chair. "Right this way, Arryn, and let me treat you to a mug of hot cocoa."

As soon as the door closes behind them, my attention snaps to Damien, who drops to his knees beside my chair and cups my cock through my pants. He drags his hand along my length as I groan, rolling my hips into his touch. "You are going to get me into so much trouble," I mutter as he leans in and nips my bottom lip before giving me an insistent kiss.

"You can cheat and take your name off the naughty list, I won't tell," he teases, and I laugh as he drops onto all fours and disappears under the table. "Dam—" My words are cut short as he yanks my chair forward, causing the edge of the tabletop to jab

138

my ribcage. He pushes the tablecloth over my lap, and I can't see him... can only feel his hands as they slide up my thighs.

"Fuck," I moan as he unbuttons my pants and slides my zipper down, pulling out his prize.

"You're so fucking big," he purrs as a drag of wet heat meets the tip of my cock, and I moan louder as he chuckles. "Someone's sensitive."

"It's like you've put a blindfold over my eyes, Damien." His chuckle forms, low and raspy, deep in his throat as he takes the head of my cock inside his mouth and gives me a gentle suck, and my head falls against my shoulders as my hips snap forward, wanting more. Every sense is heightened as fingers wrap around my shaft, swirling his tongue as he pumps me slowly.

My knees spread further, my eyes rolling into my skull at the warm swipes and insistent draws. "Fuck, that's amazing," I groan as I reach under the table to find his head. His tail grabs my wrist and holds it still, not allowing me to take charge as he sucks me deeper into his mouth. I try to thrust forward again, but he expects it and uses his other hand to pin my hip in place.

"Goddamn it, Damien, you're driving me crazy," I mutter as I struggle against his grip, wanting nothing more than to fuck his mouth until tears streak his cheeks. Instead, he holds me there, sucking me with a patient, controlled rhythm. "Think you can take charge, do you?" I murmur as he hums a contrite little sound that tells me he does. His lips tighten and

Letters to Satan

his suction increases, and I struggle, needing more, as spit slicks down the length of my dick.

Footsteps in the hallway cause me to freeze. "Damien," I hiss, but he only releases a quiet moan as he sucks the tip of my cock. "Damien!" I fight against his hold, then sit up straight as the door swings open and Arryn and Cadbury return.

If I thought this would be enough for Damien to stop, I was sorely mistaken.

Cadbury nods as he heads into the hallway, and Arryn glances around before sinking into her chair. "Where did The Lucifer disappear to?" she asks right as he takes a few more inches in his mouth, not even attempting to hide the slick sounds of his sucking.

"Something important came up," I say with the straightest face possible, a huff of breath blowing against my groin as he laughs. "How was... *ngh*... how was your tour of the workshop?" I clear my throat as Damien's tongue slides along the base of my cock, slathering me in his spit that drips a slow trail down my length.

"Delightful! It really is fascinating to see how things are done up here."

"Fascinating," I parrot. It's all I can manage, because my brain has been reduced to mush. Damien's lips seal around me in a tight ring and he slides down until the head of my cock bumps the back of his throat. "Very... very fascinating."

"Um, yes, well... When you're ready to implement your plan, just send word directly to me in a letter and we'll finish coordinating."

G. Eilsel

"Very well... a letter." Arryn stares at me, bewildered, for a few seconds, because I've turned into a bumbling idiot, and she's no doubt waiting for me to be a gentleman and escort her out. A quiet gag sounds from under the table, and I cough again to cover it. "Excuse me for being rude, but stress has me under the weather. If you'll step into the hall, Cadbury will see you out."

"Very well. I look forward to hearing from you, Santa." She has that sultry expression on her face once more, and I jolt as Damien lightly sinks his teeth into my shaft.

"Likewise," I breathe, and she finally, *finally*, walks out the door and Cadbury's voice fades down the hallway as he escorts her. My chair pushes away from the table with a loud, protesting screech as I toss the tablecloth aside, exposing Damien. He's beautifully desperate, on his hands and knees, flushed face glistening with saliva and cock pressing against his pants. The whimper he releases is obscene as he humps the air, the fabric soaked with his pre-cum until a clear, glossy thread precariously hangs.

"Get out here," I growl, standing with my spit-slicked cock jutting out. He crawls out and kneels in front of me, rubbing his cheek against my erection and spreading the sticky dampness between us. He tugs at my pants until they bind around my thighs, then ducks his head and sucks one of my balls into his mouth.

141

Letters to Satan

"Did you enjoy that? Listening to me talk to her while she had no idea you were under there, choking on my cock?"

"Mm hmm," he moans, slurping and licking along my sac, tugging the skin between his lips.

"And what if you'd been caught?"

There's a wet pop as he releases me, resting his cheek against my hip as he stares up at me with those honey-brown eyes full of lust. "Then I guess she'd have to decide whether she wanted to watch or get the fuck out while I finish what I started."

"Cheeky thing," I mutter, dragging my thumb over the mess on his chin, tilting his face even higher. "On your feet." He scrambles to stand, and I lift him with eager hands, throwing him over my shoulder. Needy little slut that he is, he moans and grinds his hips, rutting his cock against me as he shamelessly searches for relief. My free hand sweeps over the tabletop, clearing a spot before I drop him on it.

He's nothing more than putty in my hands as I shove his shoulders, his back hitting the table with a thud. I circle around to the opposite side and pull him towards the edge, watching as his head drops to hang freely. "Good boy," I purr as his lips pop apart, waiting obediently. "Your mouth is going to be occupied, little prince. If you need to stop, tap my leg three times, okay?"

He barely has time to nod before I thrust, burying myself in the heat of his mouth as he coughs in surprise. I hold there, with my cock lodged in his throat, and lean in to drag my fingers through the

142

G. Eilsel

damp spot on his pants. "Such a leaky boy, with that pretty little cock getting so wet."

My hips pull back and he sucks in a quick breath before I drive forward again, loving the pulse of his muscles spasming around me. He tries to catch suction, but my movements are too rough as I plunge into his mouth, and he pops off with a wet slurp every time. I work his zipper open and free his cock, his red skin flushed and his crown slick with his arousal.

My palm drags over his cheek, massaging the spit into his skin. "I'm going to fuck your throat now, sweet Damien." His watering eyes widen as I press forward, meeting the resistance of his muscles as his body tries to push me away. "Relax," I murmur, rubbing my hand along the column of his neck. "Relax and let me in."

He takes a stilted breath through his nose, and I groan as the muscles yield, allowing me to break through their barrier. My eyes are locked on his neck, watching the bulge of my cock stretch him. With a snarl, I give a final thrust, and I'm seated inside him so deep, his lips push against the skin of my groin.

"You're doing so good, taking all of me like this," I murmur as I pull back a few inches and thrust forward, and his body tightens in a muffled cough.

I place my palm on his throat as I do it again, punching my hips with more power this time. "Fuck, I can feel my cock inside that slender little neck. It barely even fits, but look at how well you take it, sitting perfectly still like a good boy." Movement catches my eye, and I glance up to watch his dick

Letters to Satan

bounce, a small burst of white leaking from his slit and rolling down his length.

"You're about to come just from being used, aren't you?" He chokes on another cough as I slide in and out of his throat, squeezing his neck from the outside as the grip around my cock tightens. "Such a good little cocksleeve, letting me use all these holes however I want. I'm going to fill you from every end, little prince, until it drips out of you, and then I'll do it again. You'll be too limp—too *used*—to do anything but fucking take it."

A muffled cry vibrates up my length as he thrusts into the air. A deep chuckle leaves me at his needy desperation, and I speed up, holding his throat for support as I fuck it. "That's right... you'll be laying there, too blissed out to even move, and I'm just going to keep fucking you until your holes are all stuffed and raw."

His hips jerk up once, then a second time, and on the third, he falls apart. He's as beautiful as a work of art as his back arches and he lets go, eyes squeezed closed and pink lips stretched around me. Streams of his release roll down his cock as it twitches, pitiful wails muffled between his lips as I stare, enraptured.

"Gods, you're fucking perfect," I rasp as I thrust faster, and spit explodes from the corners of his mouth as I drive into him, flooding his flushed face in rivers.

Covered in his own thick release, his cock is still hard, and I groan as my every muscle tightens. "That wasn't enough for the greedy little prince, was it? You want more." His body jolts as I drive between his spit-slicked lips, clear strands webbing between our bodies, soaking my crotch and his face. My head throws back as I mindlessly fuck into him, fighting my need to let go and holding out until I feel like I'm being ripped apart at the seams.

With a shout, I bury myself as I let go, gasping in relief as the tension wrings itself from my muscles. My hand squeezes over his neck, feeling the pulses of my cock as my cum floods his throat. His name becomes a chant as I thrust forward, trying to get even deeper, until the table scrapes over the floor with the power of my thrusts.

His hips are lifting off the tabletop again, desperate and ready to blow. Once the final waves of my orgasm fade into aftershocks, I pull out and he fills his lungs with a drawn-out gasp. Tears and spit streak his cheeks, his skin is flushed and angry, and his lips are swollen with droplets of cum leaking from the corners.

"Wrecked for me... so fucking beautiful this way," I whisper, rubbing my hand down his filthy face as he stares at me, adoring. "You just sit right there, sweet boy."

Circling the table, I grasp his legs and drag him to the far side, licking him clean and savoring the taste of his release while he struggles to push deeper into my mouth. "Watching you come like that? The way you lose control is the sexiest thing I've ever seen," I murmur as I tease him.

"Please, Nik," he whines, his voice throaty and used. "I can't take any more... just give me what I need."

Letters to Satan

"Since you asked so nicely," I say, holding his eyes while I drop my head, taking him all the way to the base. He whimpers, a hand threading into my hair, then gives a single pump into my mouth. Another thrust and a loud, pleading moan tears its way from his throat, and his knees lift, the bottoms of his feet landing on the table. I suck harder as he thrusts with more power, his tail thrashing as he fucks into my mouth.

"Daddy, please... please, Daddy, please," he whimpers, his entire body quivering as his knees fall apart, hips tensing as his mouth hangs open in a silent shout. The base of his cock thumps against my lips as he spills over my tongue, gasping and moaning as his thighs quiver and shake.

When his body slacks against the table, I suck up and off his cock and let it land on his stomach. I hover over him with my hands on either side of his head, and his sated, hooded eyes cause my heart to thunder inside my chest. It's like we don't even need words as he parts his lips, ready and waiting as his cum slides from my mouth, dripping onto his tongue in a creamy puddle.

"Good boy," I whisper, watching his tongue swirl his release, holding it for me obediently until I press my lips to his. I kissing him lazily, like we have all the time in the world, as both of our pulses slow. I pull back and rest my forehead against his, terrifying, forbidden thoughts racing through my head. "Come on," I say, voice rough, "let's get you cleaned up."

CHAPTER 12

TELL THE TRUTH AND SHAME THE DEVIL

Damien

The days blend one into the next, a filmstrip of memories and experiences flashing on a reel fast enough that I can no longer distinguish between them. Any denial that I'm neglecting my duties has long since gone out the window. *Neglecting* is an awfully loose term for the way I'm pretending to be nothing more than a bedwhore for Nik, but I suppose it works as good as any.

No, I've been having a grand old time, hiding from Xalreth so I don't have to listen to his accusations. "You've forgotten your purpose in

Letters to Satan

coming here, Lucifer," and "We cannot continue to waste time here when the realm needs you, Lucifer."

And the fact that those comments are true? Neither here nor there, I assure you.

Every night, my desire to return home shrinks, and my longing to stay intensifies. Niklaus's stress grows more and more by the hour, and the guilt that swarms inside me might as well be the size of a mountain from how it weighs me down.

An unprecedented, unfamiliar sensation has crept over me until it is all-consuming. It's sticky, and uncomfortable, and I don't have the first clue what to do about it.

I want to... h... h...

Gods, I can't even say it.

Help.

I cringe at the mere thought of it, but I've moved past the stage of denial and am settling—very hesitantly, might I add, with lots of appropriately panicked kicking and screaming—into acceptance. The initial glee that came from my rebellious group of Hellves and our sex toy workshop has darkened and twisted, turning into absolute shame for the grief I'm causing Niklaus.

We spend hours every night wrapped up in each other, both of us indulging in the rare moments where we get to pretend the rest of the world isn't crashing down around us. Admissions pass from his lips to my ears, voicing that his biggest fear is missing his Christmas Eve deadline. A fear that is coming to life right before both our eyes.

Seven days.

G. Eilsel

A mere week exists to uncover a solution. Only I don't have to search for the problem.

I *am* the problem.

He just doesn't know it.

The nervous energy in my mind searches for an outlet, and I find myself wringing my hands as I step into the workshop. The Hellves are hard at work, the room almost overflowing in the products they've spent the past week creating. "There you are!" Jujube shouts, clearly blind to visual cues as he runs over to my side. "We need to discuss implementation."

"Implementation?" I echo, glancing at him in question.

He nods enthusiastically, gesturing around the room like a tiny Vanna White... Vanna Slight, perhaps. "We will have to figure out the best way to load these into Santa's sack..." I mentally give myself a pat on the back for not even *considering* letting that chortle leave my throat. "... before he leaves on Christmas Eve. Only a few elves are allowed in the loading area, much less to touch the sack..." Another subdued laugh gets squashed in my mouth.

I'm the Devil.

Sue me for finding balls funny.

"... and I'm not optimistic about convincing any of them to do our bidding."

"Uh huh," I murmur noncommittally, my brain spinning at a million miles an hour, a wave of panic replacing my dim amusement as the gravity of the situation sinks in.

Letters to Satan

When we first got here, I was so proud of this plan. I've done lots of things over my life that are questionable at best, but this? Loading the Santa up with a bag full of dildos and cock cages and sending him out into the world?

How fucking funny it was going to be, knowing I'd gotten a leg up on him. The crown jewel of my fucked-up arsenal, gleaming and obscene, standing defiant at the top of the trophy case.

Oh, how we planned on hearing the uproar from the masses, waiting as people opened gifts to find a silicone cock instead of a boring day-planner on Christmas morning.

How hilarious it would be to imagine Brenda's face when she had neon purple anal beads—aptly named Grapes of Wrath—in front of her stuck-up husband and the fight that would follow.

How side-splittingly entertaining it would be when Maxwell blushed and tried to hide the nipple clamps behind his back. *They aren't mine!* he'd argue, but everyone knows in the history of humankind, that argument has never worked. They'd yell and scream and not speak for hours, and it would ruin their holiday.

How absolutely delightful it would be to see them all curse Christmas...

Curse Santa.

And here I am, safe and cozy in his home, taking advantage of every kindness he's offered me, ready to sit back and laugh as the chaos imploded. It was supposed to be a crowning victory in my time as Lucifer.

G. Eilsel

But now...

Now, it suddenly doesn't feel very funny.

Now it feels wrong.

Because I don't want to hurt Nik, not anymore. The image of his pain, the way the blow would shatter his impenetrable exterior... the thought alone makes my breath catch in my throat. Instead, I want to protect him, and help him, and maybe, just maybe, love him and see if he might find a way to love me back.

"We... we shouldn't do this," I whisper, but Jujube keeps talking as though he doesn't hear me... and maybe he doesn't.

"What I was thinking may work best is if we swap out *our* gifts with the others after they've been sorted and before they are loaded onto the sleigh. It'll be a bit of a time crunch, and we'll have to be silent while we do it, but I think we can pull it off if..."

"I don't want to do this," I say louder, but he still just keeps fucking talking.

"... and once they're on the sleigh inside the sack, no one checks anything again and there's no way anyone would catch us at that point."

My mind swims and I push my palms against my temples, shaking my head as it all just gets to be too much. The guilt, his grating, know-it-all voice, the images of a broken Nik.

"Just... just stop!" I bellow, power making my voice flood every corner of the room, and his eyes widen as each head in the workshop whips to me. "What the **FUGIO** are you all even doing?! Why are

151

Letters to Satan

you even here?! Why did you agree to sabotage a man that's so *good* to you?!"

Their mouths all hang open now, too, and complete, uncomfortable silence fills the shop as my temper flares out of control. My magic blasts out of me in waves, turning the air oppressive as it sparks across their skin.

In my rage, I pick up a giant green Grinch dildo and a small riding crop, holding them up with a shake. "No, I need *someone* to explain this to me! I'm The Devil—making mischief is what I do. It is *expected* of me. But why—"

"Damien!" Xalreth snaps from the back of the room, but I ignore him, my anger too powerful to put aside.

"People have been judging me as *trouble* for as long as I can recall, like there's nothing more to consider. Even before I became the Lucifer, everyone knew not to cross evil little Damien. Hellish, and terrible, and godda—" I catch myself before the censoring does, and I use the interruption to take a deep, shuttering breath. "If I want to cause chaos in the North Pole, if I want to make The Santa's life a living Hell, it makes sense. It's what everyone already expects of me. But *why*—"

"Why indeed, Damien," a quiet voice behind me interrupts, and I freeze, shock-still, as I twist to meet the fury of Niklaus's green eyes. The world plummets, the ground underneath my feet slipping away as I fall. Down, down, down I go, wind rushing my ears as I realize with absolute, devastating certainty that any chance I had of fixing this is gone.

G. Eilsel

I am now truly, utterly, *deservedly* alone.

"Everyone out." His voice is dangerously low, his impenetrable eyes not veering from mine. And I've seen these emerald eyes in various forms of anger and frustration…. of sadness and hopelessness, but not hard and empty.

Never like there's no emotion left in them.

"S-S-Santa—" One of the elves stutters, but Niklaus's temper explodes.

"*OUT!*" Rage burns across his face as he roars, so stark I can almost see the flames. "Out! Every single one of you, get *out*!" I swallow roughly as he crowds me, stepping backward until my legs hit the table, but he doesn't stop. He keeps moving forward until he's flush against me and the edge of the tabletop bites into my thighs.

"Nik—" I start, cursing under my breath when I lift my hands and realize that the toys are still in them. I fling them to the ground and grab onto his shirt. "Nik, listen. You have to listen to me. Give me a chance to explain."

He has to… right?

Because that's how the story goes.

The evil prince meets the good, kind man who shows him how to love. Teaches him he's been worthy of love this whole time. It's sappy and romantic, and bloody uncomfortable with all those *words* and *feelings*, but it's what happens.

They always get their happily ever after.

Always.

Only this doesn't feel very much like happily ever after. It only feels like *too late.*

Letters to Satan

His eyes are hard as granite, as though I could chisel a piece right from their surface, and the hurt on his face is enough to break me in half. We're alone in this room now, the door bolted shut and the stifling tension pressing on us.

When he finally speaks, his voice is flat, devoid of any emotion. It's like speaking to an artificial version of himself, his words as cold and lifeless as the wood he's carved from. "This was your plan, then? To sabotage me?"

"At first," I admit, and I hate myself for the way his eyes close for a few seconds, like the pain is too much, and he's trying to separate himself from it. "But then—"

"You were... what? Stealing my work force and causing me to get further behind, distracting me at night so I wouldn't see past your lies?"

"Nik, I'm sorry—"

"One thing, Damien," he growls, low and controlled and goddamned *devastating*, as he fists my shirt to pull me closer. "One fucking thing was all I ever asked of you—give me time to prepare if you're going to break my heart... and you didn't have the decency to grant me that single kindness."

"It's not like that, Nik, please allow me a chance to—"

"I want you gone." His voice is impersonal as a stranger, as frigid as the snow outside, and his eyes are steely and determined. "It was foolish of me to believe that I was anything to you, and I want you to leave."

"No, no, no... let me fix this, let me—"

G. Eilsel

"There is nothing to be fixed!" He snarls as he gets too close and brushes his lips against mine, releasing a helpless, defeated sound as his arms bind around me and he kisses me with bruising pressure.

All at once, he releases me to slump against the table. "You will be gone by morning." He turns his back to me, storming towards the door.

"Nik, don't walk away from me... I know you don't believe me, but I want you... I want *this*..."

He whirls to face me, a dangerous gleam in his eyes. "Oh, poor little prince is going to miss being fucked by his big Daddy, is that it? Let me give you one for the road then," he sneers as he rips the button clear off my pants and shoves them down my legs. He grabs a cage off the table and clicks it in place around my cock as I can't do anything but stare, speechless. He whips me around towards the table, shoving my face down onto its surface so my ass is exposed to him.

"This is what you wanted, right? Reap the harvest of your schemes and tell me how much you enjoy it." He grabs a dildo and shoves it into my mouth, and I gag at the taste of the silicone in my mouth. "Get it nice and slick, *Lucifer*, or else you're going to feel it."

The use of my formal title is like a blade to my gut, and I try to twist to look at him, but he pins me in place. I could use my power to free myself, but I don't know if I can handle the brokenness on his face again.

He rips the toy from my mouth, and I sputter as he moves it behind me. "Nik, I didn't mean to," I

Letters to Satan

whimper as he circles my hole. He pauses, a bitter laugh tearing from his lips.

"You didn't mean to? Which part happened by accident, Lucifer? Was it the recruitment of my elves to help in your plot? The stealing of my materials and commandeering of this room? Getting me further and further behind schedule?" The tip of the toy breaches my rim, and I gasp as my back arches. "Or was it playing my emotions like they were nothing more than some shiny new toy for you to get excited over, Damien? Tell me, how long did it take for the novelty to wear off? For you to get *bored* and move on without a care in the world to how I might feel?"

"Nik," I whine as he inches the dildo deeper. Even in his anger, he's careful not to hurt me, and the tattered shreds that remain of my heart shatter at the realization. "It was a mistake."

"All of this was a mistake," he snarls, and I call out as he works it the rest of the way inside me. We've fucked so much over the past few days that I've needed little prep, and he knows that. Knows he isn't hurting me, but I don't want him in anger.

Don't want his last memory of me to be one of such spite when it could've been such beauty.

My cock throbs, trying to thicken but being stopped by the cage, as the metal bites into my flesh. "Everything we've done has been a mistake. You are nothing more than a *mistake* and I regret every second of it."

And there it is.

The heart that even I didn't know existed cracks, straight down the middle. Pain like I've never

156

experienced bleeds into my body, and I just want to disappear.

I don't want to be *me*, not anymore.

"Pitchfork," I whisper, and Nik becomes perfectly still behind me. He could be a marble statue, not even a twitch of his fingers for a few long breaths.

He eases the toy from me and slams it onto the table beside my face with such force the metal surface dents under his fist. The suction cup grabs and I stare at the dildo swinging like a metronome before me.

"But do you know what my biggest mistake was, Damien?"

"Nik—" I plead, eyes stinging as his mitt of a hand keeps me in place, my cheek grinding into the cold metal.

"My biggest mistake was not slamming the door in your face the minute I saw who darkened my doorstep. I should've run, should've told you to go back to the pits of Hell where you belong, but instead, I welcomed you into my home. Let myself believe you could *care.*"

"Nik," I beg, "Please, Nik, I care, I do." *I care so fucking much.* His imposing presence backs away from my body, and I'm left a whimpering mess, pants around my ankles, dildo waving in the wind beside me.

"Don't leave me," I whisper, hot tears blurring my vision, but even I know it's too late for that. It's a silly request from a silly man, and he pays it no mind. Without a word, Niklaus turns and flings the door

Letters to Satan

open, storming out into the workshop and leaving me here. Alone.

Always alone.

My legs fail and I crumble to the ground, curling into a ball and hugging my knees to my chest. Exposed to the world in more ways than one, I don't have the energy to care anymore. I sense Xalreth's presence as he runs into the room, but all I can manage is to hug tighter and do something I haven't done in my many long years in this life.

I cry.

G. Eilsel

CHAPTER 13

WHAT IN THE HELL?

Niklaus

Thud. Thud. Thud.

The incessant knocking on my door jars between my ears like a bomb, and I stare into the fireplace, wondering if they'll find their answer in my silence and leave.

"Sir?" Cadbury calls from the other side, and I sigh, because I've known him long enough to realize that hoping he'll walk away unanswered is no better than wishing the snow outside would turn to sandy beaches. He's a persistent shit. As if to drive the point home, he knocks again. "Sir, I know you're in there, and I've brought your dinner. May I enter?"

Letters to Satan

With a deep, drawn-out sigh to voice my displeasure, I open the door, and he offers me a tentative smile, carrying a tray loaded with a thick stew and fresh bread. "Thanks," I say, the word barely more than a grunt as he sets it on the table.

"Sit," he commands, and I raise my brow at his tone. "With all the respect owed to your position," Cadbury leans forward and grabs my arm with a soft squeeze, "and as your *friend*, I'm telling you to take a few minutes and have dinner. You've hardly touched your food in two days, and you haven't spoken a word to anyone."

Two days.

It's been two long, painful days since Damien ripped my fucking heart in half. Two days since I realized he'd been leading me on the whole time, toying with my affections like they were nothing more than a piece of paper for him to crumble in his fist and toss into the trash. Forty-eight hours of restless energy and no sleep and grasping for solutions to my problem that I can't seem to find.

For the first time in history, Santa won't be ready for Christmas.

What a fucking failure I've turned out to be.

Golden crust crunches between my thumb and pointer finger as I tear off a piece of bread, dunking it into the rich broth and watching as it seeps into the soft middle. I shove the bite into my mouth, recognizing the texture and flavor of the food, but it's still barely more than ash on my tongue.

The swallow I force is a struggle, the bread taking a few tries to find its way down. "They are gone?" I finally ask, my voice rough with lack of use.

"Yes, sir. The Lu—" My eyes snap to his and he abruptly pauses before clearing his throat, apology written in his grimace. "I watched them step through the portal myself, sir."

"And the elves that were involved?"

"They've been taken off the workforce and isolated to their quarters for now, until you decide what is to be done with them." This is the part of the job that I'm no good at, because no matter how much their betrayal hurts, I don't want them punished.

Not how I want to see him punished, I think, and my hand flies to my chest as I rub at the phantom pain there. What sort of idiot have I turned out to be, falling for someone who could so clearly never actually love me back?

Thinking I could tame the Devil himself.

My nostrils flare as the wildfire of my anger threatens to take over once again, but I quell it, pushing it down until it's nothing but an ember. "What do you think I should do with them, Caddy?"

He's thoughtful as I force myself to take another bite that's no easier to stomach than the first. "Extra hours in the workshop would help get caught up."

A spiteful laugh leaves my throat as I stare into the fire once more. "There's no getting caught up at this point. I wasted too much time, and now I'll be written into history as the only Santa to miss Christmas."

Letters to Satan

"We'll make it work, sir. Even if we have to move gifts around and reduce what people are getting, we'll make sure that everyone has a Christmas."

"I don't deserve you, Caddy," I say, so quiet it's barely heard over the crackling logs, and I swallow again, forcing past the lump in my throat. "I don't deserve to hold this position, or the trust that has been placed on my shoulders. Once this Christmas is done, we'll start the search for my replacement."

"But sir—"

"I'd like to be alone now, if you don't mind."

He hesitates, watching me stir my spoon methodically through my soup, not bothering with the pretense of taking anymore bites. His hand lands on my shoulder, but I don't meet the scrutiny of his gaze. "Of course, sir. I'll be close by, should you need me."

And with that, he leaves, and I'm alone.

Again.

My fingernails scratch through my beard, which has gotten scruffy in the aftermath of all the chaos. The usual scissors-to-a-football-field level of grooming standards I have for myself have fallen to the wayside, and I look as unkempt as I feel.

G. Eilsel

Disappointed is far too mild a word for the contempt I have for myself in this moment. Disgusted might come close.

Repulsed might come even closer.

Anger surges deep in my gut again, but there's nowhere to direct it other than to myself. It's my fault he stayed, because I took one look into those honey brown eyes and thought... what if?

Every time his name crosses my mind, it festers and boils like a wound I refuse to treat. It's become an integral moment in my life that I can't outrun.

I'll now measure life in years of B.D. and A.D.

Before and After Damien.

The dim light filtering through the window casts long shadows on the desk, mirroring the melancholy that has settled over me like a heavy blanket. I haven't left my office in days, and I've simply accepted that whatever's going to happen, will.

The elves may appear eternally young, but their youthful looks belie the weight of their long lives and countless experiences. I'm hoping that by staying out of the way, they can navigate my blunders and prevent Christmas from being a complete disaster this year.

Amber liquid sloshes in my glass as I stare at it, the firelight shining through and transforming it into the same color of his eyes. My knuckles whiten as I tighten my grip around it, and a furious, defeated snarl crawls from my throat before I can stop it. Glass shatters and flames erupt as I hurl the cup into the

Letters to Satan

fire, the accelerant sending a wave of heat to wash over my face.

My chest heaves on an angry inhale, the fire's dance reflecting in my eyes. I can be pissed off at Damien all I want to be, but the one truly deserving of my fury is me.

What will be left for me after this?

A sudden commotion from the workshop causes me to pause, and I glance at the time with a frown, seeing that it's past dinnertime. With the amount of overtime Cadbury said he'd have elves working, it makes sense that they'd be in the shop this late, trying to make up for the mess I've put us in. I sigh, sinking back into my seat.

The noise doesn't die down, though, instead building until it's at a level I've never heard it. Voices boom through the hallway, and I freeze, every one of my senses on high alert. They rumble low, nothing like the high-pitched, slightly squeaky timbre of the elves.

Deeper, louder, scratchier, and... almost demonic.

My nostrils flare, my temper a powder keg ready to ignite, and I burst from the door, my feet heavy with rage, pounding against the ancient wooden floors as I storm into the hallway. The sight that greets me at the shop entrance is so shocking that I screech to a halt, my breath catching in my throat.

Every inch of the workshop... every surface of my sanctuary... is filled with demons.

Hundreds of them, not a single one identical.

G. Eilsel

Shades of red, orange, a sickly green, and even one so dark he seems to suck in the light that surrounds him. Mostly large, but a few smaller bodies mixed in, and every variation imaginable. Cloven feet, silky fur instead of skin, and bat wings blur into a nonsensical image, and then I see the cyclops, and my brain refuses to absorb anything else.

Pandemonium ensues as they prance around the workshop, cackling as they dart about in a chaotic carousel of motion. Surprise still has me frozen in place until my eyes land on *him.*

So beautifully horrible that my heart breaks all over again.

Blond curls curtaining his forehead as his tail whips about, he orchestrates the whole thing like some sick conductor in that hideous fur coat. They follow him blindly, *adoringly*, and I feel it, then.

The last sliver of hope I must've held onto.

It dies a slow, painful death at his hands.

It wasn't enough that he made me believe he cared... wasn't *enough* to splinter my heart into a million pieces that he so carelessly threw into the wind, but now this?

To destroy the last bit of joy remaining in my life?

Honeyed eyes meet mine from across the room, and that last threadbare string holding me together snaps. Tears burn behind my eyes, held back by nothing more than sheer willpower, as I stare at the man I thought I loved.

The man who took everything from me.

Letters to Satan

The world seems to blur at the edges as my gaze sweeps the room, like my anger has clouded my perception. My fists clench, nails digging into the flesh of my palms, and my insides are aflame, the inferno fueled by the betrayal that has shattered my trust. Each breath I take feels heavy and labored, suffocating and desperate and *maddening*.

I invited the Devil into my home, and he showed me who he is.

It's time to return the favor.

Power swirls around me as I call on the magic that my position grants me, churning inside me like a tempest, its energy rippling across my flesh.

A few of the demons stop their rampage, their wicked laughter cut short as they turn my direction, their gaze now steadily fixed on me.

I see their fear.

Smell it.

Relish it.

My lip tears up in a sneer as I step forward, slamming my hand towards the ground as the first wave drops to one knee before me. A torrent of magic, more potent than anything I've ever wielded, seethes within me, itching to unleash its wrath upon those who dared invade my sanctuary.

My vision is blurred with the golden hues of my power as I open myself to it, more bodies hitting the ground in submission as I take deliberate steps through the room. The world narrows to a kaleidoscope of pinpricks, my ears buzz with a deafening drone, and I press onward, driven by an anger so white-hot that it seems to sear my insides.

The very seams of my existence are bucking and straining against the magic.

Let it take me, I think, but even my thoughts don't sound like my own.

"Niklaus." A voice nudges at my consciousness, but I push it aside and force another difficult step forward, drowning in my desire to destroy them all.

"Nik!" Something wraps around my neck and yanks with a surprising strength, and my teeth are bared as I whip my face down and come nose to nose with Damien. "Nik, stop! You're hurting yourself... *please* stop."

"Why do you care?" I wedge a hand between us and hurt flashes through his warm eyes as I shove him away. Surprised at how easily I'm able to fling him to the ground, I hesitate. The sharp crack of his body hitting the floor, followed by his pained cry, sends a wave of ice through my veins.

"Nik, stop," he whispers, and I realize in that moment that it's silent in this shop, every demon yielding to my power.

Every demon.

Every one.

Even Damien, whose head is bowed as he sprawls at my feet.

"Nik, please listen to me and *look*," he begs, and the churning energy fizzles enough that the golden sparks thumping in my vision subside, and I stare at the top of his head. Moving in tiny, jerking motions like he's having to fight it, he lifts his eyes to mine. "*Please.*"

Letters to Satan

Body still frozen, my gaze darts between the creatures before me, finally noticing the elves sprinkled in among them. Some hold materials or tools, others are carting boxes of finished products. My anger shifts to confusion and more of the power I'm holding onto is released. The demons are visibly relieved as they're able to shake off the lingering effects.

"What is this?" I demand, and Damien remains at my feet, staring up at me.

"They're helping."

"Helping?" I repeat, my gaze shooting back up to the demons, half of which appear sheepish and the other half who might be questioning their life choices that brought them here.

Damien rises, but only to his knees, not taking his eyes off me. "When you said you wouldn't make your deadlines for Christmas, I... I knew I had to do something. They're all here for me, and they'll stay until everything is done."

The rest of my power fizzles out as I focus every razor-edged ounce of my hatred towards the man at my feet. "And what do you gain from this?"

Cautiously, he stands and pulls his lip between his teeth, grabbing on to my shirt and tugging me closer to him. I relent, but only a few inches, eyes still narrowed as I try to figure out his next move.

"I get to say this to you... I'm sorry for the pain you suffered at my hand. For every terrible decision I have made since I arrived here to meet you, and for every moment I spent working against you for my

168

G. Eilsel

own amusement. But most of all? I'm sorry it took me so long to realize that all those icky, tangled feelings were just... me falling in love with you."

Shock has me jerking back, and once again, hurt flashes across his eyes. But he's shown me who he is already, and I can't possibly believe this.

Can I?

"The Lucifer is incapable of love," I say, keeping my voice as emotionless as possible.

"Well," he says, placing his palms flat on my chest and giving me those soft, doe eyes that got me into this mess to begin with. "It's a good thing I'm no longer The Lucifer."

Letters to Satan

CHAPTER 14

THE DEVIL YOU KNOW

Damien

Confusion is soon replaced by disbelief, and finally, the last bit of his stifling power evaporates, and the restrictive vise on my lungs is loosened. My age, coupled with centuries of honed skills, makes me an incredibly powerful demon, even without the magic of The Lucifer behind me.

But here, in his domain?

He reigns supreme.

The raw energy that had been coursing from him was as intoxicating as it was all-encompassing. It was warm magic, sparking like tiny electric currents across the top layer of my skin, while telling me in no uncertain terms that he was comfortable holding his place at the zenith of the food chain.

He's the alpha, and I'd be a fool not to submit to his rule. Even at my peak power, I doubt I could've bested him in a direct confrontation.

"What?" he breathes, eyes searching mine. The anger is still there, raw and untamed, the distrust evident, but a flicker of curiosity peeks through the facade, offering me the tiniest glimmer of hope.

"Can we…" I push up on my toes again, trying to close the distance between us, but he doesn't give me an inch. My fist closes around his shirt, and I wrestle him closer, staring into those stony eyes, before I relent and press my lips to his, but they're stiff and unmoving.

Disappointment chokes me as I drop to my feet and awkwardly chew on my bottom lip, trying to read his expressionless face. "Can we go somewhere and talk?" His jaw clenches as he grinds his teeth, and I swallow past the emotion in my throat. "Give me a chance to explain, and if you… if you still want me to leave, I will. I'll leave and I'll never come back, but I'm begging you to hear me out."

His gaze flicks up to the room full of demons, not a single one trying to hide their intrigued staring. "And them?"

"Xalreth and Cadbury can make sure everyone stays on task." His eyes dart over to the corner, another flare of surprise when he sees his number two and mine—well, the demon who *used* to be

Letters to Satan

mine—standing together amiably, planning the logistics of the workshop. "Nik, please."

Our eyes lock again, holding each other captive in a silent battle of wills. The seconds stretch into an eternity, until a curt nod, a mere flick of his head, breaks the spell. With a sharp turn, he walks towards his office, leaving me standing there, the sting of his indifference hitting like a slap. Xalreth finds me as I gesture at the hallway to let him know where I'll be, then hurry after Niklaus.

Orange flames flicker shadows across his imposing form as he sits, fingers steepled in front of him, and I take a minute to soak in his appearance. Dark bags hang under his normally bright green eyes, dull with exhaustion and missing their usual fire. His beard is scruffy, and his hair is wild, like his hands have pushed through it enough to almost make it stand on end.

Guilt claws at me, its tiny teeth sinking into my gut with each accusing glance from his piercing eyes.

He was mine to have, mine to hold on to... until I took it a step too far.

Still, despite how battered he looks, there's an aura of undeniable power that makes him appear invincible. Like he could be cracked and bent, but never broken. Never diminished or destroyed.

Not like me.

"What do you have to say for yourself?"

Palms sweating and pulse racing, I meet his eyes and take a steeling breath before I lay it all out on the line. "My arrival here was driven by nothing

G. Eilsel

more than sheer boredom and a thirst for something new. Life had turned monotonous, and when another of those candy-striped letters landed on my desk, it was... a convenient distraction."

"A distraction," he repeats, his voice flat and emotionless, and I nod, barely able to meet his eyes.

"We got here, and everything was just so... innocent. Corruptible. You have to understand, in Hell, every soul has their own nefarious plans and hidden agendas... even the nice ones. Everyone is scheming and plotting, and there's constant rebellion and fighting for the sake of conflict. Here at the North Pole, it was organized and, and... *peaceful*, and hundreds of years of instinct kicked in before I could stop it. There's no excuse for my actions other than I saw a chance to cause chaos, so I did."

"By hijacking my elves to make sex toys." His voice rumbles deep from his chest, his anger escalating with each word as I slowly nod.

"But then we started spending time together, and you were... nice. You didn't view me as The Lucifer, or a ruler to overthrow, or a tool to gain favor. I wasn't an opportunity. For the first time in a very long time, you saw me as Damien. Just *Damien*... just me. And I was so fucking hungry for that, Nik. I was starving for someone to look at me and see the person instead of the position."

His eyes soften a fraction as he leans back in his chair, his chest rising on a deep breath. "I never saw you for what you could offer me, Damien," he says quietly, and my heart breaks a little further.

Letters to Satan

"I realize that now," I whisper, biting at my lip to fight the sting behind my eyes. "The better I got to know you, the more ashamed I felt about what I was doing. You're just so goddamned *good*, Nik. You're good in ways I could never imagine... in ways I couldn't accomplish if I dedicated a century to trying. But I wanted to try... I wanted to try for *you*, and I went to shut it all down because I knew what the truth would do to you."

Risking another glance at him, I find the same blank slate on his face, and that sting behind my eyes grows to a sharp ache. "You'd hate me, and I couldn't stand that. I couldn't fucking handle the idea of you hating me, so I went to put a stop to it, and it was too late. You were there, and you hated me."

He tracks the rogue tear that's slipped free, and I furiously wipe it away, unable to hold his intense stare. "I've never hated you, Damien."

"You do," I insist, despising the break in my voice as I scrub at my face. "You hate me and you're going to tell me to leave, and I'll never see you again."

"You're no longer The Lucifer?" he asks, interrupting my self-pity party as I glance up and shake my head. "Why not?"

I swallow hard, and slowly, I force the words out. "Because if I'm The Lucifer, I have to be in Hell... and if I'm there, I can't be here with you." His eyes land on mine, some of that fire igniting behind them. Rage and frustration or something else, something sweeter, I can't yet tell.

"Here with me?" he repeats, and still, I'm unable to read him.

G. Eilsel

"My heart can't be in the position if it's trapped here with you, now, can it?" His only reaction is a slight lift to his brow, and he ignores me, which, I won't lie, really fucking stings.

"If you are no longer The Lucifer, why did the demons follow you here and agree to work? What do they possibly gain from following a former leader?"

I mean, ouch.

Exhausted, a slow sense of defeat has washed over me, and I slump in my chair, giving a vague wave of my hand. "I have been in office a long time, Nik, and despite what you might think about me, I've always been a fair ruler. I listen to problems, and, when I can, fix them. The inhabitants of Hell hold a great deal of respect for me, *former* leader or not."

He stares at me for a while, face unyielding, and the last tiny spark of hope starts to die in my chest as he takes a breath and pushes out a drawn-out, heavy sigh.

Rejection.

This is rejection, and I can hear it in his breath and taste it in the fucking air between us. It's rejection, and now... now I'll have nothing.

Be nothing.

"Come here," he finally says.

"What?" My head snaps up so fast I'm surprised it doesn't bounce.

"Come here, Damien." His voice is soft but insistent, and I force my shaky legs to stand and walk around the desk, never taking my eyes from his as he swivels in his chair to face me. "Closer," he demands, and I step forward between his knees. He shoves my

Letters to Satan

jacket off and tosses it away, and I somehow find the indignation to scowl. His hands wrap around my thighs, and I have to grab his neck for balance as he hoists me to straddle his lap.

"Look me in my eyes and tell me what you want from me."

My hands tremble as they hold on to him, inching closer. "I don't want anything from you, Nik. For the first time in my life, I don't want to take. I want to give. I want to give you the entire goddamned world, and all I ask in return is that we go back to pretending you could ever love something as evil as me."

"Pretending?"

"Just let me believe it, Nik... let me believe I'm good enough..."

"Damien," he breathes, brushing my lips in a kiss. "You think I could fake this?" Sheepishly, I stare at him, before a very unmanly sniffle leaves me. Yeah, we're going to erase that from this memory like it never happened.

Nik smiles. "Sweet Damien, I started falling in love with you the moment I first glimpsed that snarky smile and saw straight past that mask you wore. You might think you have the world fooled, but I've seen your heart. You have been it for me from the day we met."

"But I fucked it all up," I whisper, another stupid tear breaking free as my frustrated hand goes to erase it, only to be caught mid-air in his giant fist.

"You did," he agrees, kissing the salty trail off my skin. "And now you're going to have to work hard to make it all better."

A ragged sound climbs from my throat, desperate and relieved, as I push my lips to his, a hint of salt on top of all that sweetness. And like it set off a chain event that can no longer be stopped, we're touching everywhere. His hands in my hair, mine on his shoulders, chests and hips moving together, and tongues twisting as we fight to get even closer.

"Can you forgive me?" I ask, breathless, against our kiss, and he nods, but doesn't separate us long enough to answer. My palms land on his chest and I force myself back. "Words, Nik. I need to hear this. I need you to tell me I haven't lost you."

A smirk spreads over his lips as he nudges his nose with mine. "I know you aren't trying to dom me right now."

My mouth twitches in a tiny smile. "Never."

"That's my boy," he whispers, the sound a low rumble in his throat, before his gaze turns intense, his fingers idly tracing the outline of my lip. "I won't insult you by lying to you and pretending you didn't hurt me, Damien. I may not be as old as you, but I consider myself to be an extraordinarily reasonable man. Until you come into play, and then logic abandons me altogether. But mark my words," he says, and my heart thuds again at the warning in his voice, "if you are using me, or if this is a new game you're playing, there will not be another chance. This is it, Damien."

Letters to Satan

"I won't need another chance." Tucking my face into his neck, I throw myself against him. "I won't waste this one, I swear it," I whisper.

"My little prince," he purrs, and goosebumps rise on my skin from the warning in his tone. "Just know that I would search every corner of the realms to hunt you down, and there wouldn't be a single shadowy corner that would protect you from my wrath. Don't forget that."

Holy fuck, the threat should not be so sexy, but my cock bucks in my pants at the growl of his voice.

Our mouths find each other again, and my fingers work their way under his shirt, running my palms and fingertips along the heated skin of his abdomen as I rock into him. A pitiful whimper leaves me when he grips my hips and pushes me back, my lips chasing his. Reluctantly, I climb to my feet at his sharp glare.

"Pants off, Damien," he commands, undoing his button and zipper and pulling his thick cock out as he waits for me to obey.

"Are you not going to be naked, too?" I pout, yanking my shirt off and working on my pants.

His grin is downright filthy as he strokes himself. "You like how slutty it makes you feel when I take you with my clothes on. It's alright, Damien, you can be my little whore, and I'll fuck you raw without even bothering to get undressed." I whimper as I shove my pants to the ground, and his eyes immediately zero in on my cock.

G. Eilsel

"You never took it off?" I glance at my dick, trapped inside the cage he put on me days ago, a drip of pre-cum leaking between the wires.

"I'm not supposed to take it off until Daddy says I can." I walk over, standing between his knees again as he strokes himself with one hand and reaches up to drag his fingers over my cage with the other.

"Well, Daddy says it stays until I'm done watching you come while wearing it." I climb onto his lap, and he finally releases his cock, both of us staring as it lands in the crease of my thigh. I lean forward, my movement causing his face to twist in a contorted expression of pure pleasure. He grabs the lube from his desk drawer and holds it against my hole, and I can't help my moan when he squeezes it and shoots the gel inside me.

"Such a needy thing," he murmurs as he sets it aside and catches the dripping lube, using it to slick me up with a teasing finger.

"Fuck, I've missed you inside me," I moan as I rock on his finger, tossing my head back and letting my voice ring free at the pleasure that slingshots through my body.

He moves that finger with maddening slowness, each inch feeling like an eternity, so I try to speed things up by bearing down and pushing back, almost bouncing in my eagerness. "Someone's sensitive today." Nik leans forward and licks up the column of my neck, sucking on the skin around my Adam's apple so hard I know he's leaving behind a mark.

Letters to Satan

So much pleasure and anticipation coil in my muscles that I start to lose control of myself, gasping and moaning as I ride on his hand. He trails down to the curve of my shoulder and starts on another mark as a second finger stretches into me. Both fingers pull back until they're barely inside me, catching my rim as he slams them forward. Soon, he's thrusting into me in a steady, forceful rhythm.

My body is on fire as I press backwards into him, chanting his name as he sinks his teeth into my shoulder. "Nik!" I shout, and he freezes as my ass squeezes around his fingers, my cock pulsing and trying to fall over the edge. "No, no, no," I wail, rocking faster. He only allows a single second of this before he stops me with his other hand and pins me in place.

"You haven't been given permission to come yet."

"Please, Daddy, please," I beg, fighting to move against his iron grip.

He clicks his tongue and leans in, scraping his teeth over my ear before whispering, "If you think you'll be allowed to come without my cock buried inside that ass, you're sorely mistaken, sweet prince."

I whimper as his hand cracks across my ass cheek. "Who does this ass belong to?"

"You, it belongs to you."

Another slap, a harder one, causes me to shout. "Wrong answer. Whose ass is this?"

"It's Daddy's ass," I whine as he places his palm over my reddened cheek, soothing the sting.

G. Eilsel

"That's right... it's Daddy's ass. And what can Daddy do with this ass?"

"Whatever he wants."

"Such a good boy," he purrs, sliding his fingers from me and notching the head of his cock at my hole. There's a sting as he pushes forward a few times, my rim stretching for the sledgehammer he tries to call a cock. I drop my weight, loving the sweet ache as my body opens for him, and I slide down until he's fully seated. "God, I've missed this ass. This hole that's only mine."

"Only yours," I agree, lifting off him until just the tip kisses my hole, then sinking back down with a wet suction as we both moan.

"Damien," he gasps as he grabs my hips so hard they'll bruise, thrusting up into me as I clutch his shoulder so tight my nails dig into his flesh. I've never seen him lose control like this, tendons in his neck drawn and sweat beading on his forehead. His mouth sags open as he fucks me, digging and clawing at my skin with such force that I can only hang on.

My cries are so loud that I'm sure they can be heard down the hall, but neither of us care as he pounds into me harder. I gasp, scrambling to grab his shoulders as he stands and drops my back onto his desk. His body canopies over mine as his palm lands on my throat, cutting off my air supply and making my brain go fuzzy.

"That's my good boy," he grunts, every word punctuated with the thrust of his hips that sends papers and pens flying into a flurry. "God, look at the way you take my cock." His fingers tighten around

Letters to Satan

my neck as he uses it for leverage, skin slapping as he drives me straight to the edge.

"Nik," I rasp against his grip, "Nik, I'm gonna..." My head throws back as my spine makes a perfect arch off the desktop, and my shout is strangled as the tension all explodes out of me all at once.

"Fuck!" he shouts, cutting off my air completely as he fucks me rough, and it only heightens the orgasm that's blasting through my system. Cum shoots from between the wires of my cage, pouring in a river down the metal bars. He curses once more then bottoms out, filling me up with a long, low moan.

He releases my neck, and I suck in a loud breath, still whimpering as my sensitive cock twitches inside the restraint of the cage. When his whole body slumps and he pulls out of me, cum drips down my skin, rushing out of my worn hole in a filthy stream. We stay like this, face-to-face, as he reaches up and pushes my curls back off my sweaty forehead.

"You're staying?" The vulnerability in his eyes splays me wide open.

Oh, my heart.

"If you'll let me."

"I'm pretty sure I've made it clear by now that I'll let you do just about anything." I smile as he leans in for a sweet kiss. "There is... *one* thing we need to come to an understanding about."

Sudden nerves bite at my stomach at the serious tone in his voice. "Oh... okay."

G. Eilsel

"I am burning that ugly fucking jacket." Relief swarms through me and I bark out a laugh, and soon he joins me, resting his forehead against mine. Still grinning like fiends, he swoops me off the desk and carries me to his bathroom, where he fawns over cleaning me for the next half hour.

And as we climb into bed together, spooned up and holding on for dear life, I let myself believe that maybe, just maybe, the devil might find his happy ending after all.

Letters to Satan

CHAPTER 15

THE GIFT THAT KEEPS ON GIVING

Niklaus

"Are you sure everything is loaded?" Damien, every inch the pint-sized dictator has a group of elves beside the sleigh nodding like synchronized puppets. "You're positive? Nothing has been missed?"

"No, Luci..." My brow arches as the elf speaking sneaks a gaze towards me before clearing his throat. "No, Master Damien, we didn't miss anything. We have protocols in place that we've been following for centuries."

Oh, there's definitely a touch of haughtiness behind that one, I just wonder if...

Damien's eye twitches at the same rate as his tail.

Yep. He noticed.

"Do not sass me, little **SHIH TZU**!" Damien's eyes narrow into tiny slits as he takes a threatening step towards the workers, who scatter, and I can't help my chuckle as I walk over.

"Are you causing trouble?" I murmur, swooping in to kiss him behind his ear, and he shivers as he turns around with an incredibly innocent smile.

Terribly suspicious.

"Me? Little old moi? What is this... trouble that you speak of?" He pronounces it 'trub-lay' like he doesn't understand what it means.

There's not a soul on this planet that would believe the devil isn't a handful.

But he's my handful.

My sleigh, gleaming under the moonlight, is ready for departure, the final check completed by the group Damien so effectively scattered, leaving only the hushed anticipation of the night.

The reindeer are majestic in their crimson harnesses, the quiet jingling creating a merry tune as they shift restlessly between their hooves. An occasional, impatient bleat will ripple through the herd from time to time, the others mirroring it with their soft, downy noses shaking impatiently as they wait for their cue.

Through the cargo bay windows, the snowy landscape unfolds, fat snowflakes softly falling, a

Letters to Satan

silent, shimmering spectacle against the backdrop of a star-studded sky.

It's something I thought I'd miss this year.

Something I thought I'd have to give up forever.

Fate, however, has a wicked sense of humor, and it often throws a lifeline at us from the most unexpected places.

Thanks to the combined efforts of the elves and the demons, along with some heavy-handed managing by me, Damien, Cadbury, and Xalreth, we met our production goals with a day to spare. It left just enough time to sort and load the sleigh, and now we're ready.

The entire North Pole is exhausted, including the legion of Hellions that are staying one more night to reap the benefits of their hard labor.

My unexpected saviors.

The demons were surprisingly pleasant to work with, despite the... trouble... with the curse filter. For the first couple of days, it was non-stop chaos, a symphony of random words being shouted in every corner of the overcrowded workshop.

OSHA, forgive me.

Once they got used to it, things calmed down. There were a few pranks, a handful of arguments, but by and large, everything went much smoother than I ever expected it to.

"I have a surprise for you," I say as Damien smiles at me again, more genuine this time. From the bag at my side, I whip out a Damien-sized Santa coat—fluffy, red velvet with white fur-lined sleeves and neck. Imbued with my magic, it will keep him warm regardless of the icy winds or biting cold, at high altitudes and even higher speeds.

He grins as I slide it over his slender shoulders. "You think this looks better than my old coat? You clearly know nothing about fashion here in the North Pole," he teases, but I notice the way he draws it around him and sinks into the warmth.

"You'll need it tonight," I say as I gesture towards the ladder onto the sleigh, and his smile fumbles.

"What?"

I lean in and drop a kiss on his surprised, pouty lips. "Christmas only made it this year because of you, Damien. You better be prepared to see this through to the finish line, because I'm not going anywhere without you."

He licks his lips, then narrows his eyes, attempting to hide the way he's affected. "Are you sure this isn't an excuse to keep a closer eye on me?"

I chuckle, dropping another kiss on his temple. "A mere coincidence, I assure you."

"So, I really get to ride with you in the sleigh? With..." His already wide eyes grow even rounder. "With the reindeer?!" That makes me laugh, a rich one straight from my belly that threatens to become a stereotypical Santa laugh, and he's still doe-eyed as he stares. "But... but how does it work? There's so many houses and so little time."

I shrug, nudging him towards the sleigh. "Magic."

Letters to Satan

He climbs up, awe-struck, as the elves finish the preparations, poking and prodding at every switch and button, needing to touch everything as he explores. When we receive the final thumbs up, he grabs my hand and squeezes as I take the reins.

And then we're off.

Being a gentleman, I won't mention his rather undignified, almost childlike, squeal during takeoff. Or the way he holds onto me so tight, I'm convinced he's caused a few hairline fractures.

Once the sleigh stabilizes, he relaxes, soon becoming brave enough to hang over the sides and stare down at the landscape far below. After he does his second round of exploring, he snuggles in beside me with a sigh, and I throw my arm over his shoulders.

High in the sky, moonlight shines through the snow that falls around us, framing his features in its gentle glow. "Thank you," he whispers, so quietly I barely hear him.

"For what?" I tuck him into my side, where he nuzzles his face against my chest.

"For showing me what I was missing in life… and forgiving me when I was an idiot." He tilts his head up, and I oblige him with another soft kiss. "For taking care of me and for teaching me what it's like to be loved."

"I have one more surprise for you. Reach into my sack…" I ignore his delighted snort of laughter, "… and pull out a present."

"Oooh, is it for me?" he asks, diving towards the back and pulling out a gold-wrapped box.

"Sort of."

He cocks a brow at me, and I wave at the box. "Open it."

Paper goes flying as he rips into the gift, and his mouth sags as he stares into the packaging. "Is that..."

"A red-gemmed Decked Halls buttplug? Yes, Damien, it is." He tilts his head at me in question, and I laugh again. "I had a discussion with the elves, and we figured out that people have been asking for more... risqué gifts for centuries, and they've always been ignored because it wasn't 'proper.'"

I lean in and grab his chin, forcing his eyes to mine. "And then a cheeky little Devil forced his way into my life and made me realize that sometimes, a bit of debauchery isn't a bad thing."

His grin stretches all the way across his face, wrinkling the corners of his eyes. "So, what you're saying is Santa's bringing sex toys this year?" Another loud laugh booms from my belly as the first town comes into sight in the distance.

"This Christmas, Santa's doing things just a little differently." I hesitate, and his eyes find mine in curiosity. "And as it turns out, I might need someone to head that department... if you know of anyone who might be sticking around for a while."

His smile is sweet, lacking the normal sass that he carries, and he leans in for a kiss that I happily give him. "As it turns out, I think I might know just the guy."

We kiss for a few minutes as we edge closer to civilization, and I begrudgingly separate us and

Letters to Satan

gesture at the box in his hand. "There's lube in the side compartment. You're to put that in and leave it until we're back. I want you stretched and ready for me."

He reaches over, finding the bottle and shaking it at me. "You going to come down my chimney, Santa?"

"Only if you stay on the Naughty List, Damien." We both laugh at that, because there's no risk of his name being moved to the nice list. He's the Devil... he doesn't need a title to be mischievous and sneaky, crass and demanding, but most of all?

He's mine.

Horns and all.

ABOUT THE AUTHOR

G. Eilsel started writing under this pen name in early 2024, publishing works in two genres she loves: eccentric novellas and MM romance.

Her writing puts a focus on sarcasm, snarky humor, sometimes horrible puns, and steamy scenes that'll make your momma blush. Expect heavy spice, in any sort of variety you're looking for-sweet, emotional, depraved, or downright questionable.

Some of her books are one-handed reads with minimal plot, others are more intricate stories that weave themselves through her brain and demand to be put on paper. Angsty and emotional, light and

Letters to Satan

giggle-inducing, and everything in between can be found between the covers of her books.

She doesn't take herself too seriously, throwing pieces of her humor and quirky personality in her writing. If she can't live up to her title of a One-Handed author, then maybe she can at least make you smile.

Want to get in touch?

Find her on Facebook and Instagram
or email g.eilsel.author@gmail.com

G. Eilsel

OTHER BOOKS BY G. EILSEL

One Handed Holidays - Crossed Swords Edition

Raising Hell: A Spicy MMM Novella
Letters to Satan: A Spicy MM Novella

Get Your Rocks Off

First Verse: An MM Romance
Chorus: An MM Romance
Second Verse: An MM Romance

One Handed Holidays

Come To Cupid: A Spicy Novella
Irish Cream: A Spicy MFM Novella
Down the Rabbit Hole: A Spicy Dark Novella
Mother F*cker: A Spicy Reverse Age Gap Novella
Shadow Daddy: A Spicy BDSM Novella
Raising Hell: A Spicy MMF Novella
Land Ho!: A Spicy Navy Novella

Made in United States
Cleveland, OH
27 December 2024